Memories . . .

His lips touched her hair, and there seemed to be a tremor in his hands. "It was dynamite," he whispered. "You were fire and honey in my arms, and I remember crying out because the pleasure was an agony."

She tore herself out of his arms and got behind the table, looking across at him with wide, wounded eyes. "Go away!"

His eyes were dark with remembered desire, his face shadowed by the light behind him coming through the curtains. "I will, but the memory won't," he said huskily.

"You used me," she whispered brokenly, letting the hurt show involuntarily, seeing how his face hardened. "It wasn't until . . . until it was all over, until it was too late, that you told me the truth. I hated you then and I hate you now. I'll hate you until I die, Keegan Taber!"

Dear Reader,

Welcome to Silhouette! Our goal is to give you hours of unbeatable reading pleasure, and we hope you'll enjoy each month's six new Silhouette Desires. These sensual, provocative love stories are both believable and compelling—sometimes they're poignant, sometimes humorous, but always enjoyable.

Indulge yourself. Experience all the passion and excitement of falling in love along with our heroine as she meets the irresistible man of her dreams and together they overcome all obstacles in the path to a happy ending.

If this is your first Desire, I hope it'll be the first of many. If you're already a Silhouette Desire reader, thanks for your support! Look for some of your favorite authors in the coming months: Stephanie James, Diana Palmer, Dixie Browning, Ann Major and Doreen Owens Malek, to name just a few.

Happy reading!

Isabel Swift
Senior Editor

SDRL-7/85

DIANA PALMER
Eye of the Tiger

Silhouette Desire

Published by Silhouette Books New York

America's Publisher of Contemporary Romance

SILHOUETTE BOOKS
300 East 42nd St., New York, N.Y. 10017

Copyright © 1986 by Diana Palmer

All rights reserved, including the right to reproduce
this book or portions thereof in any form whatsoever.
For information address Silhouette Books,
300 East 42nd St., New York, N.Y. 10017

ISBN: 0-373-05271-5

First Silhouette Books printing April 1986

All the characters in this book are fictitious. Any
resemblance to actual persons, living or dead, is purely
coincidental.

SILHOUETTE, SILHOUETTE DESIRE and colophon are
registered trademarks of the publisher.

America's Publisher of Contemporary Romance

Printed in the U.S.A.

Books by Diana Palmer

Silhouette Romance

Darling Enemy #254
Roomful of Roses #301
Heart of Ice #314
Passion Flower #328
Soldier of Fortune #340
After the Music, #406

Silhouette Special Edition

Heather's Song #33
The Australian #239

Silhouette Desire

The Cowboy and the Lady #12
September Morning #26
Friends and Lovers #50
Fire and Ice #80
Snow Kisses #102
Diamond Girl #110
The Rawhide Man #157
Lady Love #175
Cattleman's Choice #193
The Tender Stranger #230
Love by Proxy #252
Eye of the Tiger #271

DIANA PALMER

is a prolific romance writer who got her start as a news-paper reporter. Accustomed to the daily deadlines of a journalist, she has no problem with writer's block. In fact, she averages a book every two months. Mother of a young son, Diana met and married her husband within one week: "It was just like something from one of my books."

One

Eleanor Whitman saw the red Porsche sitting in the driveway and deliberately accelerated past the small shotgun house on the mammoth K.G. Taber farm outside Lexington, Kentucky. She knew the car too well to mistake it, and she knew who would be driving it. Her heart quickened despite all her efforts at control, although she had every reason in the world to hate the car's owner.

Her slender hands tightened on the steering wheel and she took slow, deep breaths until they stopped trembling, until the apprehension left her huge dark eyes.

She had no idea where she was going as she turned onto a long, calm avenue with big, graceful shade trees down the median. Lexington was like a series of small communities, each with its own personality and neighbors who were like family. Eleanor often wished that she and her father could live in town, instead of on the farm. But the house was theirs rent free as long as her father lived, a kind of fringe benefit for employees of the elder Taber. Dozens of employees lived on the mammoth farm: carpenters, mechanics, farm laborers, a veterinarian and his assistants, a trainer and his assistants, a blacksmith...the list went on and on. The farm had two champion racehorses, one a Triple Crown winner, and a prime collection of purebred black Angus bulls as well. It was a diversified, self-contained property, and the Tabers had money to burn.

Eleanor's father was a carpenter, a good one, and he alternated between repairing existing buildings and helping put up new ones. He'd had a bad fall and broken his hip three months ago, an accident from which he was only just now recovering after extensive physical therapy. And the Tabers had been keeping him on, paying his insurance and all his utilities despite Eleanor's proud efforts to stop them. They were holding his job open and looking after him like family until he could work again, which the doctors said would be soon. Meanwhile, Eleanor took care of him and petted him and was grateful that the fall hadn't killed him. He was all she had.

In her teens, Eleanor had loved the big white house with its long, open porches and wide, elegant columns. Most of all, she'd loved Keegan Taber. That had been her downfall. Four years of nursing school in Louisville had matured her, however, and her decision to accept a position at a private hospital in

Lexington was a measure of that maturity. Four years ago, she'd succumbed to Keegan's charm and accepted one tragic date with him, not knowing the real reason he'd asked her out. She'd hated him ever since. She spoke to him only when he was impossible to avoid, and she never went near him. It had taken her a long time to get over what had happened, and she was only now starting to live again.

What puzzled her was that Keegan had been acting oddly ever since her return. He didn't seem to mind her venomous looks, her dislike. And it didn't stop him from visiting her father at the house, either. The two men had become close, and Eleanor wondered at the amount of time Keegan had been spending with her father lately. Keegan seemed to have plenty to spare, and that was odd because his business interests were diverse and made many demands on him. Now that his father, Gene Taber, was feeling his age, Keegan had assumed most of the responsibility for the farm. Keegan was an only child, and his mother had died many years before, so there were only the two men at Flintlock, the huge estate with its graceful meadows and white-fenced lushness.

Flintlock had been the site of a miraculous occurrence during the settlement of Kentucky. During a fight between pioneers and Indians, the settlers ran out of water. In a daring act, a pioneer's wife—some legends said Becky Boone herself, wife of Daniel— led the womenfolk of the encampment down to a bubbling stream to fetch water in their buckets. And, miracle of miracles, the Indians actually held their fire until the women were safely back with their menfolk. There was a historic marker at the site now; it was in the middle of a cattle pasture. Tourists still braved the bulls to read it.

Eleanor drove past that pasture now and remembered going to see it with Keegan long ago. How naive she'd been, how infatuated with him. Well, she was over it now; Keegan had given her the cure. But the experience had almost killed her. Certainly she'd been dead inside for a long, long time. Thanks to Wade, however, she was beginning to feel alive again.

Wade had been invited to the house tonight for the first time to meet her father. Eleanor hoped that Keegan didn't have any standing plans to visit with Barnett Whitman that evening to play their regular game of chess; she wanted her father and Wade to get to know each other. Keegan, she thought with a flash of irritation, would only be in the way.

Wade Granger had become someone special in her life, she mused, smiling as she recalled their first few meetings. He'd been a patient and had formed an attachment to her, as patients sometimes did to their nurses. She'd laughed off his invitations, thinking he'd get over it when he left the hospital. But he hadn't. First he'd sent flowers, then candy. And she'd been so shocked at the royal treatment, because he was as wealthy as Keegan, that she'd dropped her guard. And he'd pounced, grinning like a cartoon cat, his dark hair and eyes sparkling with amusement at her astonishment.

"What's wrong with me?" he'd asked plaintively. "I'm only six years older than you are, eligible, rich, sexy. What more do you want? So I'm a little heavy, so what?"

She'd sighed and tried to explain to him that she and her father weren't wealthy, that she didn't think getting involved with him would be a good idea.

"Poppycock," he'd muttered dryly. "I'm not proposing marriage. I just want you to go out with me."

She'd given in, but she'd invited him home for a meal instead of accepting his invitation to go nightclubbing. She thought if he saw how she lived, and where, it might cool him off.

He was a nice man, and she liked him. But she didn't want to get involved. Keegan had cured her of being romantic. Now she knew all too well the consequences of giving her heart, of trusting a man to return her love. She knew how cold the ashes of a love affair could be.

Her father had no idea of the relationship she'd had with Keegan, and she wanted it to stay that way. It had only been one date anyway, one magical night when she'd believed in fairies. What a pity she hadn't been levelheaded. But she'd been flattered by Keegan's sudden interest, and she hadn't questioned it at all. She certainly hadn't suspected that Keegan was only using her to get back at the woman he really loved. She often wondered what had become of Lorraine Meadows. Petite, blond Lorraine with her Park Avenue tastes and no-expense-spared upbringing. Keegan had announced his engagement to Lorraine the morning after his date with Eleanor. She remembered hearing it and bursting into tears. Keegan had tried to talk to her, and she'd refused to come out of her room. What was there to say, anyway? He'd gotten what he wanted.

But although the engagement made social headlines, less than two months later the couple quietly dropped their marriage plans and went their separate ways. It was incredible to Eleanor, who was in nursing school in Louisville by then. She felt Lorraine would have been the perfect mistress for Flintlock. These days, of course, Lorraine Meadows was never mentioned. Keegan was apparently playing the field now, according to local gossip.

Eleanor drove around for half an hour or so and then went home, thinking Keegan had had plenty of time to finish his business with her father. But he was still there. And she didn't have the time to avoid him any longer, not with Wade coming at six-thirty. It was four now.

She pulled up at the front steps, behind the classy Porsche, and cut the engine. Nurse's cap in hand, she walked wearily in the front door and fought down the rush of excitement that seeing Keegan never failed to create.

He was in the living room, sitting across from her father and looking out of place in the worn, faded armchair. He rose as she entered the room, all lean muscle and towering masculinity. There was an inborn arrogance about him that actually rippled the hair at her nape, and he had a way of looking at her with narrowed eyes and a faint smile that brought the blood to her cheeks. His flaming red hair had a slight wave in it, and his eyes were as blue as a summer sky. His cheekbones were high, his features sharp and cutting, his mouth thin and cruel and oddly sensuous. He looked lithe and rangy, but she knew the strength in that slender body. She'd seen farmhands underestimate it, to their cost. She'd underestimated it herself, once. But never again.

"Hello, Keegan," she said in greeting, her voice calm, confident. She even smiled at him as she bent to kiss her father on the forehead. "Hello, darling, had a nice day?"

"Very nice." Her father chuckled. "Keegan drove me into Lexington to the therapist. She says in another month I'll be back on the job."

"Lovely!" Eleanor laughed.

Keegan was watching her closely, as usual. He got lazily to his feet. "I've got to run. Eleanor, your father and I can't find that last cost estimate he did on building my new barn. Do you know where it is?"

So that was why he'd been here so long. She smiled at her own wild thoughts. "Surely. I'll get it for you."

She went into her father's small study and reached up on a high shelf for the box where he filed his bills and important papers. Her breath caught when she got down to find Keegan lounging in the doorway, his blue eyes narrow and intent on her slender body in its neat white uniform.

"Did I shock you?" he asked with a taunting smile. "It's been some years since I've managed that, hasn't it, Ellie?"

"I don't like that nickname," she said coolly. She avoided his gaze and sat down behind the desk, riffling through her father's papers until she found the estimate. She pulled it out and extended it toward Keegan.

He jerked away from the doorframe and took it from her. "How long do you plan to hold this grudge against me?" he asked softly. "It's been years."

"I have nothing against you, Mr. Taber," she said innocently.

"Don't call me that," he said curtly. "I don't like it."

"Why not?" she asked with a bland expression. "You're the big boss, aren't you? We live in your house, provide you with entertainment—of all sorts," she added bitterly, meaningfully.

His thin lips compressed. He rolled the paper in his hands, making a tube of it. He stared at it, then at her. "You came back. Why?"

"Why not?" she asked, lifting her eyebrows mockingly. "Did you expect me to stay away for the rest of my life to spare you embarrassment?"

"You don't embarrass me," he said shortly.

"Well, you embarrass me," she returned, and her brown eyes glared at him. "I hate the memory, and I hate you. Why do you come here?"

"I like your father," he replied. His chin lifted slightly as he studied her. "He was injured on the job. I've been keeping an eye on him since you couldn't."

"I know that, and I'm grateful. But he's almost healed...."

"He plays a good game of chess," he said. "I like chess," he added through pursed lips, smiling thoughtfully, and his gaze was thorough and bold.

"You like strategy," she returned. "I remember all too well what a wonderful manipulator you are, Keegan. You're great at getting people to do what you want. But not me. Not anymore."

"You just can't give me credit for an unselfish motive, can you?"

"Ah, you forget," she said silkily. "I know all about your motives, don't I?"

His blue eyes glittered at her like sun-touched sapphires, and his face tautened. "My God, haven't you ever made a mistake in your unblemished life?"

"Sure. With you, that night," she replied heatedly. "And the irony of it is that I didn't even get any pleasure out of it!"

He seemed to go rigid with that accusation, and his face actually colored. "Damn you," he breathed furiously, crushing the tube in his lean hand.

"Does that rankle? Forgive me for trampling on your vulnerable male pride, but it's the truth." She pushed back a wayward lock of her soft, brown hair. "I gave you what I'd been saving all my life for a man I loved, only to find out when it was too late that it was a ruse to make Lorraine jealous, to get her to marry you! Did you ever tell her just how far it went, Keegan Taber?" she demanded, burning up with the years of bitter anguish. "Did you?"

"Lower your voice," he growled. "Or do you want your father to hear it all?"

"Wouldn't he have a sterling opinion of you then?" She laughed wildly. "His chess buddy, his idol. He doesn't know you at all!"

"Neither do you," he said shortly. "I tried to explain it to you then, and you wouldn't listen. I've tried since, several times. I even wrote you a letter because you wouldn't talk to me."

"I burned it, unread," she replied triumphantly. "What could you have told me that I didn't already know? Lorraine called me herself. She was delighted to tell me all the details...." Her voice broke and she turned away, biting her tongue to keep from crying out, the pain was so fresh. She took a steadying breath and rubbed the back of her neck. "Anyway, as you said, it was all over a long time ago. I'll even forget it one of these days." She glanced at his rigid figure. "Wouldn't you like to go and manage your farm or something? I've had a long day, and I still have to cook supper."

He was silent. She heard him light a cigarette, heard the snap of his lighter as he pocketed it. She thought he'd stopped smoking, but apparently her father hadn't known that he'd started again.

His voice sounded bleak when he spoke again. "I didn't realize until afterward how much you cared about me. And by then it was too late to undo the damage."

"I hope I wore your conscience thin," she replied. "You can't imagine what you did to my pride. But at least I didn't get pregnant." She managed a laugh, folding her arms over her breasts. "Whatever happened to your intended, by the way? I expected you to drag her to the altar the minute she opened her mouth and said yes."

"I don't want to discuss Lorraine!"

Of course he didn't; he'd loved the socialite to distraction, despite her wearing ways. She shrugged, as if it didn't matter, and went to the doorway.

"If those papers are all you needed, I'll excuse myself. I have to get my man a decent supper."

He stared at her, his eyes searching and curious. "Your man?"

Her dark eyes widened. "Shocked? I do realize you think you're a tough act to follow, but I can't believe you expected me to moon over you for the rest of my life. Yes, I have a man," she lied. Well, Wade was a man, and he might be hers someday. "He's gorgeous and sexy and rich as sin."

"Rich?" he returned.

"You probably even know him. Wade Granger?"

His face flooded with angry color. "You little fool! He's what's known as the crowd Romeo! The only way he hasn't been caught doing it is hanging from a limb!"

"How erotic!" she murmured, smiling sweetly. "I can hardly wait!"

"Damn you, will you listen to me? He's just out for a good time!"

"So were you." Eleanor folded her arms across her breasts. "Go ahead, boss, warn me about the consequences. Lecture me on rich men who look upon less wealthy women as fair game for their unsatisfied desires. You sure ought to know what you're talking about.''

He looked as if he might blow up any minute, a redheaded stick of dynamite looking for a match. Even his freckles seemed to expand.

"Eleanor...!"

She knew the tone, but it didn't intimidate her anymore. "Now, don't get all worked up," she advised, smiling. "We don't want your blood pressure shooting up, do we, you poor old thing?"

"I am not old," he replied through clenched teeth. "I'm barely thirty-five!"

"Oh, but you're thirteen years older than I am," she reminded him. "Definitely a different generation," she added on a sigh, studying him. "Too bad I was too smitten with you four years ago to notice. But I'm all better now. You'll be relieved to know that I don't have any inclination to chase after you these days. Doesn't that make you feel better?"

He didn't look confident, or enthusiastic or particularly happy. He stared at her for a long time. Then, "Wade is two years older than I am," he pointed out in a strained tone of voice.

She shrugged. "Yes, but he has a young mind." She grinned. "And not a bad body, to boot." She pursed her lips thoughtfully. "A Romeo, you said? How fascinating. I can't wait to see how good he is...."

He whirled on his heel and stormed out the door without another word. Eleanor had to smother a giggle. Well, so much for his overbearing arrogance, she thought with a trace of cold pride. At least she could handle herself now; she could protect herself. And she might need that ability, because he had a slightly possessive attitude toward her. She didn't want that; she didn't want the risk of running headlong into him again. Part of her remembered too well the vulnerability of loving him. She wouldn't be that stupid again. And why should he be worried about Wade? It probably irritated him that she might wind up in bed with someone else.

Good, she thought as she went to her room to change. Let him worry. It would be small compensation for the anguish he'd caused her with his manipulations!

She got ready for dinner, dressing in a pair of lavender slacks, a striped crinkle-cloth blouse and sandals. She peeked in the living room on her way to the kitchen.

"Wade's coming to supper," she announced, grinning.

"Is he?" her father asked mildly, studying her. He grinned back. "So I finally get to meet him, do I?"

"He won't take no for an answer." She laughed. "I gave up."

"Just as well, the flowers were taking over the house." He frowned, looking so much like a mirror image of Eleanor except for his silver hair and wrinkles that she smiled. "Did you and Keegan have words?"

Her eyebrows arched. "Why do you ask?"

"He came out looking like a thunderhead, muttered something about a meeting and dashed out. It's our chess night, you know."

"Oh, I forgot," she replied honestly. "I didn't remember."

"You don't pay a lot of attention to him these days, do you? Used to be wild about him, too. I remember how you cried when he got engaged. You went rushing off to nurse's training in Louisville that same week." He started to fill his pipe, aware of her sudden color. "I don't think it's just to see me that he's starting hanging around here so much, Eleanor."

"Well, don't make the mistake of thinking he's mad about me," she replied. "I know better."

He met her gaze. "He's been hanging around here longer than you realize," he replied. "You haven't noticed."

"I don't want to notice. Please don't play Cupid, darling. Keegan doesn't interest me that way. Not anymore. Now, Wade," she murmured dryly, "is another matter."

"Do you think he'll keep coming when he sees where we live?" he asked bluntly.

"Of course," she said with a grin. "He's no snob."

He shifted in his rocking chair and set it into motion as he lit his pipe. "I'll wait and find out for myself, if you don't mind."

"If you think we need improvements, ask your friend the farm tycoon," she told him. "Use your influence."

"I wouldn't dream of it!" he sputtered, glowering at her. "And you might remember that his daddy made his money the hard way. He wasn't born into money, he earned it. The Taber farm is... Where are you going?"

"I've heard this sermon before." She sighed. "I know all about the Tabers. More than I want to know. I have to get dinner."

He studied her stiff back. "You could be a little more hospitable to my chess partner," he told her.

"Oh, I'll strain a muscle being hospitable, you just watch. I'll even curtsy when he walks in the door."

"Don't get smart," he grumbled.

"Okay," she promised. "I'll treat him with all the respect due his age. After all, I am a mere child by comparison." She turned and went into the kitchen. "I'm making spaghetti tonight, if that suits you."

"Suits me fine. Will it suit the snooty dinner guest?"

She glowered at him from the kitchen doorway. "Shame on you. Just because he has money doesn't make him a snob."

"Yes, I could say the same thing about Keegan, if you'd listen."

She stuck her tongue out at him.

"Why do you dislike him so?" he asked unexpectedly, his eyes narrowed.

What could she say to that? Telling him the truth was out of the question, and nothing short of it would convince him. She leaned forward with a conspiratorial smile. "He has freckles," she whispered. "I hate freckles."

And while he was laughing at her cheek, she vanished into the kitchen.

Two

___

Wade was right on time, and Eleanor met him at the door with a bright smile. She had expected to find him wearing slacks and a shirt, as Keegan frequently did when he visited them. But Wade was wearing a very trendy navy-blue blazer with white slacks and a white shirt and tie, and he looked taken aback by Eleanor's neat slacks and blouse.

"Sorry, love, am I overdressed?" he asked apologetically, looking briefly uncomfortable, then even more so as his gaze wandered around the hall, taking in its far-from-recent paint job, worn linoleum and single light bulb hanging bare from the ceiling.

"We're a little primitive around here," she said with a faint smile. "The house was given to us rent free by the Tabers due to the length of my father's employment here. We tend to forget how it looks, but there's never been any reason to update it, you see...."

"Was I criticizing?" he said quickly, and smiled to soften the words. "My world is a bit different, but that doesn't make it better, now does it?" He chuckled.

"No," she said with a laugh. "You're a nice man."

"That's what I've been trying to tell you." He sighed.

She stood back to invite him in, feeling underdressed and underprivileged, even though she knew he hadn't meant to make her feel that way. "Won't you come into the living room and meet my father?"

She led him there, swallowing her embarrassment at the shabbiness of their furniture. The living room needed painting, too—why hadn't she noticed that before now? And the rug—oh, Lord, it was in rags! She hadn't paid the slightest attention to the condition of the house since she'd been back. Helping her father since his accident and holding down a full-time job of her own left her just enough time to keep the house clean and neat. And there hadn't been any company to speak of, except other farm employees who were friends of her father...and Keegan, who never seemed to notice where he was, making himself right at home in castle or hovel alike.

Her father would be wearing that sweater with the hole in the sleeve, she reflected, groaning inwardly. He had better ones, but that was his favorite. Smiling, Barnett Whitman extended his hand to Wade, not seeming to notice that he looked positively ragged in his old baggy trousers, faded print shirt and slippers.

"Nice to meet you, Mr. Granger," he said easily. "Sorry I'm not getting up, but I've had some trouble with my hip and sitting down feels better."

"Yes, your daughter was telling me about your fall," Wade replied. "I hope it's better."

"I'll be able to go back to work next month," her father assured him. "The Tabers have been wonderful to me, to us."

"I know the Tabers," Wade said. "Keegan's a character, isn't he?" he added conversationally. "Quite a guy."

Her father immediately brightened. Anyone who liked Keegan was instantly a friend, Eleanor thought with bitter irony.

"Keegan often plays chess with me," Barnett Whitman said proudly.

Wade raised an eyebrow and grinned. "I can't imagine him sitting still that long. He always seems to be on the run, doesn't he?"

"In a dead heat," Barnett agreed with a smile. "But he's a good chess player, for all that."

Quickly Eleanor took Wade's arm and said, "Shall we go into the dining room?" to prevent her father from further extolling the virtues of the one man she wanted to forget. "I hope you like spaghetti, Wade. I was on seven-to-three today, and I didn't have a lot of time to prepare."

"Spaghetti is fine," Wade told her. "I should have brought a bottle of Chianti to go with it. Or a nice rosé. What do you have?"

Eleanor stared at him. "I beg your pardon?"

"Wine, darling," he said.

"Oh!" She felt her cheeks grow hot. "I'm sorry, we don't drink."

"I'll have to take you in hand and corrupt you, you innocent little thing. Shhh, we don't want your father to think I'm a rake," he added in a stage whisper.

Her father, liking this obvious attention, grinned as he sat down. Eleanor smiled as Wade seated her, but she felt oddly uncomfortable, as if her social graces were nonexistent. Without meaning to, Wade made her feel like a country mouse.

It wasn't the most successful evening Eleanor had ever had. She felt uncomfortable, although her father did his best to liven things up. By the time dinner was over and Eleanor had served up her special homemade apple pie with ice cream, she was more than willing to show Wade to the door.

He shook hands with her father and walked out onto the porch with Eleanor.

"Not a wild success, was it?" he asked with a rueful smile. "I'm sorry, darling, did I hurt your feelings?"

"Yes, you did," she said, surprised at his perception. "But it's not your fault. It's just...I guess I felt the difference in our situations...."

"You little snob," he accused her lightly.

She blushed furiously. "I am not!"

"I think you're charming, Eleanor Whitman," he said with an intent stare. "A nice person as well as a sexy lady, and I like you. I really didn't come to appraise the furniture," he added with a grin.

"Sorry," she murmured with downcast eyes. "I guess I'm a little uneasy about it, that's all."

"Stop worrying about the differences, and let's concentrate on the things we have in common. Over dinner. Tomorrow night."

She hestitated.

"Come on, sweet thing, you know you want to," he teased, bending to kiss her soft mouth gently. "Come on, go out with me, Ellie."

He made the hated nickname sound special and sweet, and she smiled dreamily up at him. He was handsome, she thought. A nice, lovely, ordinary man, despite his wealth and prominence.

"All right," she agreed.

"Good girl." He cupped her face in his hands and kissed her again, breaking the line of her lips this time. He was adept at lovemaking—it showed in the sensuous deliberation of his warm mouth. And if some spark was missing, Eleanor ignored it. It was very pleasant to kiss him. She relaxed and gave him her mouth, smiling when he finally drew back.

"Whew!" he whistled, looking breathless. "Sweetheart, you're delicious."

She laughed at the warmth in his eyes. He made her feel special, womanly.

"So innocent," he murmured. He drew her closer, nuzzling his chin against her forehead. "I like that,

I like being with an innocent woman for a change. It's exciting.''

He thought her inexperienced, and in a sense she was. But he was obviously making assumptions about her innocence that were false, and she didn't know how to correct him. She drew back, looking up at him, and her eyes were worried.

"Such a frown," he murmured. "Don't. I'm not that much a wolf, Little Red Riding Hood. I'll take care of you. I'll give you plenty of time. Now go back inside, it's chilly out here. I'll call you tomorrow, all right?''

She beamed. "All right.''

"I enjoyed dinner," he murmured. "But dessert was the best course.'' Bending, he drew her completely against him and kissed her hungrily.

She should have told him. But there would be time for that, later. And she might never have to tell him. She wasn't planning on having an affair with him, and she was sure that wasn't what he had in mind, either. He seemed to be serious. That would make a nice change. She might enjoy letting him be serious about her. She kissed him back, sighing when he released her. If only she could forget how it had felt when Keegan had kissed her....

"Good night, darling," he said in a shaky whisper, and ran down the steps to his Mercedes convertible. He started up the engine and waved, his dark hair ruffling in the night breeze as he turned the car and sped away.

Eleanor drifted back inside, feeling a little removed from reality. It hadn't been a total loss, this evening. Something wonderful might come of it.

"He's a nice man," her father said kindly. "Is it serious?"

"Serious!" she burst out, throwing up her hands. "One date, and you're wording wedding invitations!"

"So I'm anxious to see you happily settled," he grumbled, and glared at her. "Get married. Have children! I'm not getting any younger!"

"At the rate you're going, you'll outlive me!" she threw back.

He made a rough sound under his breath, got out his copy of Thucydides and began reading, deliberately ignoring her. She laughed as she went into the kitchen to wash up.

She was off the next day, having worked nine days in a row to compensate for a personnel shortage following a viral outbreak. Wade called early and had to break their dinner date because of business. He was going to be busy until the weekend, he said, but could she go to a party with him Saturday night at a nearby estate?

Eleanor held her breath, trying to figure out whom she could swap duty with to make it. Yes, she said finally, she'd work it out somehow. He told her when to expect him and rang off.

Immediately, Eleanor dialed her friend Darcy at the hospital. Darcy would take over for her, she knew, if she agreed to work Friday for Darcy.

"Can you cover for me Saturday night if I cover for you Friday night?" she asked breathlessly when her friend answered the phone. "I've got this really hot date."

"You, with a hot date?" Darcy gasped. "My gosh, I'd get up off my deathbed to cover for you if you're really going out with a man! It is a man?" she asked. "Not some sweet old gentleman you're taking pity on?"

"It is a man. It's Wade." She sighed.

Darcy paused. "Honey, I hope you know what you're doing. That isn't a man, it's a ladykiller."

"I'm a big girl now."

"A babe in the woods."

"Not quite," Eleanor said gently. "Not at all anymore."

Darcy sighed. "Well, I should be shot for agreeing, but I will. Where are you going?"

"To a cocktail party at the Blake estate."

"The Blakes own half of Fayette County!"

"Yes, I know. I'm so nervous. I thought I'd wear that little black cocktail dress I wore to our Christmas party...."

"You will not! It's three years old! I have a strappy little gray silk number, you'll wear that. It will just fit you. And I have an evening bag and shoes to match. No arguments. I'm not sending you to the Blakes' looking like something out of a Salvation Army charity store!"

That cut, because it was how Wade had made her feel. She hesitated, then gave in gracefully. She really did want to go to the party with Wade, to get a taste of that luxurious other world. And her little black dress would only embarrass him.

"Okay," she told Darcy. "You're a pal. I wish I could do something for you."

"You are," came the smug reply. "You're filling in for me Friday so that I can see that new picture with Arnold. Come over Saturday morning and we'll fix you up."

"I'll be there at nine, with coffee and biscuits from the Red Barn, how's that for true friendship?" She laughed.

"That's true friendship," Darcy agreed. "See you then."

Eleanor excitedly told her father about her plans for Saturday, then went back into the kitchen to wash the breakfast dishes, frowning when she heard a car drive up in front. She peeked into the living room, and her heart leaped as Keegan walked into it, frowning and looking worried. He sat down and started talking to her father, fortunately not glancing toward the kitchen. She quickly drew back inside.

She was too far away to hear what was being said, but she had a terrible feeling it had something to do with her. Well, let them talk, it wouldn't stop her. She liked Wade, she'd been in a state of hibernation for over a year, and she was tired of her own company. She wanted to get out and live a little before she turned into a vegetable or an old maid. And if Keegan didn't like it, that was too bad. She didn't care about his opinion. She didn't care about him, either.

The kitchen door opened, and the object of her dark thoughts came into the room, hands rammed into the pockets of his pale slacks. She glanced at him and then concentrated on her dishes.

"Can I help you?" she asked carelessly.

"Your father says you're going to a party at the Blakes' with your new boyfriend."

"So what if I am?" she asked coldly.

"You're going to be out of your league, little girl," he said bluntly. "They'll eat you up."

Her cheeks reddened with anger. She put the dish-cloth down slowly and turned to face him, her dark eyes narrow and icy. "You don't think I can behave like a lady, is that it?" she asked, glaring up at him. "Well, don't worry, Mr. Taber, you won't have to suffer my embarrassing presence. And I think the Blakes will manage not to laugh at me."

"I didn't mean... Damn it, girl, will you stop putting words in my mouth? I'm talking about Granger. I've already told you he's a wolf! A rich, sleek, well-fed wolf with a big wallet, just fishing for a naive little girl like you to warm his bed!"

She turned and stared at him. "Just like you," she agreed, and watched him explode, then turned back to her dishes. "Why are you worried about my morals? If I want to be corrupted by someone else, that's my business. Besides, I've always wanted to make love suspended from a tree limb," she added dryly.

"That's what I'm afraid," he murmured, studying her. "Eleanor, you're trying to fit into a world that has nothing of value to offer you."

"Like yours?" she asked politely.

"I'm talking about you and Wade Granger! Aren't you experienced enough to realize why he's sniffing around you?"

· He made it sound so cheap and vulgar! "I am not a tramp," she replied through clenched teeth, "despite your efforts to make me feel like one."

"When did I ever do that, Eleanor?" he asked in a deep, poignant tone, his eyes searching hers.

She didn't want to remember that night. "If you want to stay to lunch, I'm making ham sandwiches," she said abruptly, washing a plate hard enough to scrub half the pattern off.

He came up behind her, smelling of tangy cologne. She remembered the scent of it: it had clung to her body that night. It had been on her pillow when she awoke the next morning. It was a graphic reminder of her one lapse in a lifetime of sanity. The warmth of his body radiated toward her, warming her back, threatening her.

"I was careful with you that night," he said, his voice velvety rough, warm. "More careful than I've ever been with a woman, before or since. Even afterward, I was tender. I've never been able to forget it, the way you wanted me at first, the wild little shudders, the sweet cries that pulsed out of you until I hurt you."

"Please," she whispered, closing her eyes. "I don't want to remember!"

"You cried," he murmured. His lean hands smoothed her waist, drew her back so that she rested against his powerful body. "You cried when I took you, looking straight into my eyes, watching...and

I felt that you were a virgin, and I tried to stop, but I was so far gone..."

"No!" She wept, lowering her face.

His lips touched her hair, and his hands trembled. "You were fire and honey in my arms," he whispered, "and I remember crying out because the pleasure was an agony."

She tore out of his arms and retreated behind the table, looking across at him with dark, wounded eyes. "Go away!"

His eyes were dark blue with remembered desire, his face shadowed by the flash of light behind him through the curtains. "I will, but the memory won't," he said huskily.

"You used me," she whispered brokenly, involuntarily, letting the hurt show, seeing how his face hardened. "You had a fight with your sophisticated girlfriend, and you took me out to spite her. And like a fool, I thought you'd asked me because you cared about me. It wasn't until... until it was all over, until it was too late, that you told me the truth. I hated you then and I hate you now. I'll hate you until I die, Keegan Taber!"

His eyes shifted to his boots, to the worn linoleum. "Yes, I know," he said quietly.

"Will you please go?" she said in a defeated tone, refusing to look at him again. "My life is none of your business now. Nothing I do concerns you."

"Do you want him?" he asked.

She went and opened the kitchen door. "Goodbye. Sorry you have to leave so suddenly," she said with a bright, empty smile.

"I thought I was invited to lunch."

"Do you really like arsenic?" she asked with raised eyebrows. "Because I've never been more tempted in my life."

"Neither have I," he agreed, but he was studying her slender, pretty figure with narrowed, blue-black eyes. "You're exquisite, Eleanor. You always were, but maturity has done amazing things to your body."

"I am more than a body," she said curtly. "I'm a human being with thoughts and feelings and a few minor talents."

"I know that, too.... Do you fancy a guardian angel, Eleanor?"

She blinked. "I don't understand."

"You will," he said with a grim smile. "At least keep away from his apartment, can't you? I hear he has a bed that begins at the doorway."

She had to bite her tongue to keep from laughing, and his twinkling eyes very nearly threw her off balance.

"Well, that surely beats the back seat of a luxury car, wouldn't you think...?" she asked with blatant mockery.

He sighed. "You won't quit, will you? I don't suppose you'd believe me if I told you I was so out of my head at the time that I wasn't even thinking about anyone but you?"

"Right the first time," she said, grinning carelessly. "Do you want a ham sandwich or don't you?"

He pulled a cigarette out of his pocket and took his time lighting it. "I'm going to get around that wall you've built, one way or the other. You can make change on that.''

''Better buy a rocket launcher and a couple of grenades,'' she told him. ''You're going to need them.''

''You may, if Romeo gets a foot in the door,'' he said grimly. ''Don't worry your father, will you? He broods.''

''He'll have to give me up one day,'' she remarked.

''You aren't thinking that Granger might propose, for God's sake?'' he burst out, laughing coldly. ''Marry a sweet little nobody like you? Fat chance, honey.''

''I'm not your honey,'' she shot back.

''You were,'' he said, his voice rough and soft all at once, his eyes intent. ''You were the sweetest honey I ever tasted.''

''The beehive is out of order,'' she replied stiffly. ''You'll have to appease your appetite elsewhere.''

''There isn't anywhere else,'' he said absently, watching her as the cigarette smoldered in his hand, its glowing tip as red as his waving hair. ''There hasn't been for a long time.''

''I don't believe in fairy tales,'' she said. ''If you're quite through, I have things to do.''

He shrugged. ''Turned out into the cold,'' he said, watching her. ''Heartless woman.''

''It's spring, and it isn't cold. And you're one to be accusing someone of not having a heart.''

"You don't think I have one, Eleanor?" He laughed. "You might be surprised at the bruises on it."

"I would, if there were any."

"Nurses are supposed to have compassion," he reminded her.

"I have, for those who deserve it. I have dishes to wash, sandwiches to make...."

"Wash your damned dishes, and forget making any sandwiches for me," he muttered, turning to go. "The way my luck's running lately, you'd probably make mine with a live pig."

She heard the door close and went back to her soapy water. It took a long time for her heart to calm down, and she thanked providence for removing his disturbing presence. She didn't want to remember that night. Why couldn't he go away and let her forget it? Just the sight of him was a constant reminder, an eternal opening of the wound. She closed her eyes and went quickly about her tasks.

Three

Early Saturday morning, Eleanor left her father sleeping soundly and drove to the Red Barn to get biscuits and coffee for herself and Darcy. The older nurse with whom she worked was still in her housecoat when Eleanor reached her small efficiency apartment downtown.

Darcy blinked, yawning, her pale brown eyes bloodshot, her round face blank. "Coffee and biscuits," she murmured dreamily, closing her eyes to smell. "Wonderful!"

Eleanor laughed, following her friend into the apartment. The furniture was in about the same shape as that in Eleanor's house, and she felt comfortable here. Not that Darcy would ever have put on airs, even if she'd had gobs of money. The two of them had become friends years before in high school.

Darcy had done her nurse's training in Lexington, while Eleanor had gone to Louisville. But now they found themselves working at the same hospital, and it was as if the four-year absence had never been. They were as much alike as ever and had fallen back into their easy, close relationship with no trouble at all. Only Darcy had known just how deeply in love Eleanor had been with Keegan, although Eleanor hadn't told even her best friend the full extent of her stupidity. But Darcy knew why Eleanor had left town when Keegan announced his engagement because Eleanor had cried on her shoulder for hours afterward.

They sat at Darcy's small white kitchen table and ate the fluffy sausage biscuits, washing them down with coffee. It was just after nine, and the city hadn't started to buzz yet. Soon, however, the downtown traffic would be murder.

"I needed that. Thanks!" Darcy smiled.

"Oh, anytime." Eleanor grinned. "Now, about that dress . . ."

Darcy burst out laughing. "You shrewd operator! Okay, come on in here and let's look it over."

It was a dream of a dress, silk chiffon that fell in soft folds around Eleanor's slender body, a pale gray that emphasized her dark eyes and soft brown hair. She smiled at her reflection, liking the demure rounded neckline and the transparent sleeves that gathered at the cuff.

"It's heavenly." She sighed. "You're sure you want to risk this with me?"

"I got it at a nearly-new shop. It's a designer model, only worn twice. Here are the shoes and bag."

The shoes had small Queen Anne heels and straps around the ankles. They were elegant, like the tiny gray leather purse that finished the outfit.

"Wow, is that me?" Eleanor laughed at her reflection.

"Well, almost," Darcy murmured. "Sweet, your hair is dreadful. I have to get a cut today; suppose you come with me?"

Eleanor looked at the soft waves falling around her shoulders and tugged at a strand of hair that seemed more like wire. "Dreadful is definitely the word all right. Can we get an appointment for me at such short notice?"

"They take walk-ins anytime," Darcy assured her. "And some new makeup. And for God's sake, honey, a bra that has a little support."

Eleanor sighed, nodding. "I never buy under things until the old ones lose their elastic and have holes."

"You need taking in hand." Darcy shook her head. "Pretty lacy under things give you confidence. You could use a little of that!"

"I guess I could, at that. Okay. Let's renovate me."

The two of them walked to the hairdressing parlor, and the operator gave Eleanor a cut that suited her face: softly waved and very short. She looked different already, and when they went into a department store where Eleanor was shown how to apply new makeup, the transformation was complete.

"Mmmmm," Eleanor said with a smile, looking at her face in the fluorescent mirror. "Is that me?"

"It sure is, honey." Darcy laughed. "I've been wanting to do that for months. You used to be so particular about your appearance, but lately you've just let yourself go."

"I guess I have," she agreed. She touched her hair. "What a difference. Wade is going to love this."

Darcy pursed her lips. "That party's really got you perking, hasn't it?"

"Yes, it has," she admitted as they went through the women's department browsing through the latest styles. "Not that I'm trying to break into high society. That would be ridiculous. I just want to do something different, you know? My life is deadly dull. I feel like I'm growing old second by second."

"That's a laugh. You're the youngest person I know at heart. Just like your dad. How is he, by the way?"

"Getting back in shape slowly but surely, and trying to get me married off."

"Same old Dad." Darcy laughed.

"Amen."

"Wouldn't he settle for letting you have a wild, passionate affair?"

Eleanor sighed. "He couldn't get grandkids that way," she reminded her friend. "Anyway, I'm not sure I want to have an affair with anyone. Wade's wonderfully nice, and I like him a lot. But he doesn't start any fires just yet. I think that has to accompany emotional involvement, for me, at least."

"Well, personally speaking, if I were looking for a blazing affair, I know which direction I'd be staring. My gosh, I'll bet Keegan Taber is just plain dynamite in bed!"

"Oh, goodness!" Eleanor cried as her hand tore down half a dozen gowns from the rack. She colored furiously as she bent to pick them up.

"Sorry," Darcy murmured as her friend fumbled gowns back onto hangers. "I guess I shouldn't have said that, considering... But he is gorgeous, honey." She eyed her friend thoughtfully. "I bet he'll be at that party. His family and the Blakes are real friendly, aren't they?"

"Isn't this pretty?" Eleanor enthused over a pale green silk gown.

Darcy got the hint and said nothing more about Keegan. But the look in her eyes was more eloquent than words.

For the rest of the day, after she and Darcy parted company, Eleanor worried about the party. Keegan wouldn't be there... would he? She didn't want him to spoil her fun, to intrude into her life anymore. She found things to do, to keep busy. She couldn't bear thinking about it. Anyway, Wade would be with her. He'd protect her.

She got dressed early and went into her father's study, where he'd been holed up all day, to show him her borrowed outfit and her new look.

He stared and nodded solemnly. "You look just like your mother, darling," he said, smiling wistfully. "So beautiful."

"Not me. Wrong girl." She laughed. "But if you think I'll do, that's fine."

"You'll do all right. You may need a stick to beat off the boys." He lit his pipe. "Watch yourself."

"Everybody tells me that." She sighed.

"Then I'd listen if I were you." He studied her with shrewd eyes. "Remember that it's a long way from the presidential suite to the economy-class rooms, will you?"

"We're not servants," she said haughtily.

"Yes, I know that. But we're not high society, either. See that you remember it."

"Yes, Your Worship," she said, and curtsied.

"Away with you! And don't drink. You know what it does to you."

She did indeed, remembering that one date with Keegan. Her face colored, and she bent, pretending to fix her shoe strap.

"I'll remember."

"And have a good time," her father added.

"Oh, I expect to."

"And say hello to Keegan for me," he added with a twinkle in his eyes. "Didn't you know he was invited, too?"

She glared at the knowing look in his eyes, then turned as she heard a car pull into the driveway. "Well, I'm off. I'll see you when I get back. Don't be up too late, now."

He made a face at her and she closed the door on it.

The Blakes lived in a house just a little less palatial than Flintlock. It was redbrick, very old, and stood on the banks of a private lake overlooking one of the most beautiful plains near Lexington. There was rolling farmland around it, and Thoroughbreds pranced jauntily in the confines of white fences.

"Nice little place, isn't it?" Wade asked as they stopped in the driveway where a liveried chauffeur waited to drive them from the parking spaces up to the house.

"Little," she scoffed, getting into the back of the Rolls-Royce limousine. She tried to memorize every inch of the leather luxury so that she could tell her father and Darcy. It was a little like being Cinderella.

"Little compared to some," Wade replied with a laugh. Riding around in Rolls-Royces was probably nothing unusual for him. He leaned back, scanning Eleanor's ensemble. "I like your dress, darling. Silk wears well, doesn't it?"

"Uh, yes, it does," she returned. Odd that he could recognize silk; he probably wore silk shirts. Most rich men did. She remembered that Keegan had worn a white silk shirt that night....

"I like the new haircut, too," he said. "You pay for dressing, Eleanor. I like the way you look."

"I'm glad."

"Nervous?" he asked as the driver pulled up in front of the house, which was blazing with light. Exquisitely gowned women and men in black evening wear strode elegantly along the cobblestone walkway, and Eleanor did feel uneasy.

"Just a bit," she confessed.

"Just stick with me, kid, I'll take care of you," he said with a wink.

She glanced at him. Was he afraid she might slurp her soup and try to butter her bread with her spoon? She frowned. Was it a dinner party?

She asked him. "No, darling," he replied, guiding her to the front door. "It's a champagne buffet."

"With different kinds of champagne?"

"Not quite," he chuckled, pressing her hand closer. Tall, dark, good-looking, he attracted attention, even with his slightly overweight frame. And Eleanor seemed to be doing that as well. And not because she was out of place. "Champagne and hors d'oeuvres," he whispered. "Conversation and dancing. There's even a pool, if you fancy swimming."

"Well, not in my gown," she murmured demurely.

"They keep bathing suits on hand," he said, laughing. "Sometimes, they actually fit."

"I'll pass, thank you," she said with a smile.

She was introduced to her host and hostess. Mr. Blake was sixtyish, heavyset and pleasant. His wife— his third wife—was barely forty, vivacious and dripping diamonds. Their daughter was in her early twenties but already married. Her husband, an executive type, was beside her, helping to receive guests.

Fortunately no one asked if Eleanor was related to the Cape Cod Whitmans or the Palm Beach Whitmans, and she didn't have to confess that her father was a carpenter on the Taber farm. That would have humiliated her beyond bearing. She hated being an outsider. But these people and their elegant furnishings graphically reminded her of what she would be going home to. They pointed up the difference between living and surviving. And she wondered if she hadn't been better off not knowing that some people could afford trinkets like original oil paintings and velvet sofas and leather chairs and Oriental carpets and crystal chandeliers.

She had only one glass of champagne, standing rigid beside Wade while he discussed money matters with acquaintances. Conversation seemed to center around good stocks, municipal bonds, money markets, income taxes and new investment opportunities. The only investments Eleanor knew about were the ones she made on her car and groceries. She smiled into her champagne and nibbled on a delicate little puff pastry filled with chicken.

"Well, look who's arrived," murmured the older man beside Wade, glancing toward the door.

Eleanor followed his amused stare and found Keegan, in a black tuxedo, just entering the house with an elegant little black-clad brunette on his arm.

Eleanor's heart skipped a beat just looking at him. He was devastating in evening clothes, his red hair neatly combed, his patrician features alarmingly handsome. Lucky, lucky girl who had his whole attention, she thought miserably, then chided herself for the thought. After all, she was long over him.

"Isn't that the O'Clancy girl, the one who's visiting them from Ireland?"

"Yes, I think it is. Lovely, isn't she? She and her parents are hoping to work a deal with Taber, or so we hear, on a Thoroughbred of theirs," Wade murmured with a smile. "Trust Taber to come up with an escort like that. But what's he doing here?"

"He's after that new colt of Blake's—the Arabian out of Dane's Grace by Treadway. Probably Blake decided they could discuss business here as well as at the golf course." He chuckled.

Watching Keegan with the brunette, Eleanor couldn't help but wonder how many women he'd gone through since the night he'd seduced her. The thought made her go hot all over.

"Why the long face?" Wade teased, whispering in her ear.

"I don't like him," she blurted out.

His eyebrows arched. "Why not?" he exclaimed.

"He has freckles," she muttered, glowering at the redheaded man, who seemed to feel her cold scrutiny and turned abruptly. He caught her eyes across the room, and she stood there dying of old wounds, feeling the floor lurch under her feet. Her body ached; it took her last ounce of willpower to jerk her gaze back to Wade and calm her wildly beating heart. "Don't you think freckles are just horribly blatant?" she asked matter-of-factly. "I can't think why anyone would want to have them."

He laughed helplessly. "I don't suppose he can get rid of them, darling," he said.

"A likely story," she returned.

He laughed even harder and pulled her close against his side. "You bubbly little thing. I'd rather have you around than a magnum of champagne."

She knew. Oh, how she knew. She smiled up at him just as Keegan looked her way, intercepting her smile. He seemed to grow two feet and his eyes were suddenly darker, possessive. He let his gaze rove over her from head to toe, and even at a distance the look was powerfully narcotic. She avoided it this time, in self-defense.

"Shall we dance?" Wade asked. He put their glasses aside and moved her into the ballroom, where a small orchestra was playing Strauss waltzes. She moved across the floor with him like thistledown, and he grinned.

"You dance gloriously!" he said.

"Not what you expected of a nurse?" she teased. "Actually, I took dancing for three years. Ballroom dancing was part of the course. I do love a waltz."

"Then let's show them how a waltz should be performed," he murmured, and drew her around and around in the center of the floor.

Soon people were standing back to watch, because they moved as one person. He was an excellent dancer, and she followed him without a single missed step. She laughed up into his face, loving the music, feeling young again, full of life. It had been a long, bleak year, and now she was coming to life again. She closed her eyes and drifted, giving herself up to the joyous, seductive rhythm. It would have been perfect, she thought dreamily, if the arms holding her were wiry and strong, if the body against hers were lithe and lean and hard-muscled. And if the face above hers were surrounded by red hair, and if there were horrible freckles all over it....

She bit her lip. If. How long did it take a dream to die? she wondered sadly. Hers had lasted too long already.

Eleanor returned to the reality of applause all around as Wade bowed to her and led her off the dance floor. She held tight to his hand, vaguely aware of Keegan's blue eyes watching. Always watching. Why did he stare at her so? she wondered. Was it guilt?

"That was nice," she told Wade.

"I thought so, too. You're magic." He bent and brushed a kiss across her forehead. Across the room, a redheaded man clenched his fists and looked as if he could do murder.

When some of the other guests discovered that Eleanor was a nurse, she found herself much in demand to answer medical questions, none of which she felt qualified to address. She learned to excuse herself before things got too complex, and she never lacked for partners. But inevitably Keegan claimed her for a dance, and the evening turned dark.

"Having fun?" he asked dryly. "You do seem to be the center of attention."

"I'm having a lovely time," she replied. "Are you?" she added with a glance at his young partner, who was dancing with an older man and smiling at him radiantly.

"Yes, I am, as a matter of fact," he replied. "She's a sweet girl. Generous and kind and beautiful."

"Not your usual choice, but we all like a change, don't we?" she taunted.

He looked down at her possessively, his eyes charming hers as he pulled her closer, letting her feel his strength as he turned her expertly to a slow box step. "What do you know about my usual choices?" he asked. "You make a science out of trying to avoid me."

"Do I?" she asked with a carefully blank expression. "I hadn't noticed."

His eyes searched her body possessively, and the strong hand holding hers contracted a little; subtly his fingers eased between hers so that his palm meshed with her own. Her heart jumped, and his other hand felt it because it had snaked around her waist and was resting just underneath her breast.

"Not quite immune yet, Eleanor?" he asked, searching her dark eyes, her parted lips.

"I've been dancing, haven't you noticed?" she hedged.

"I've noticed you all night, and you know it. This dress is pure witchery. Where did you get it?"

She smiled. "From the Salvation Army. Isn't it nice?"

He drew in an irritated breath and turned her quickly, so she almost lost her balance. She felt his body intimately in the turn and put a little distance between them.

"Stop fighting me," he muttered.

"Am I?" She looked up into his eyes lazily. "I thought you were reminding me of my place. Do you think this scene is a little too grand for your carpenter's daughter, Mr. Taber, sir?"

"Have you been drinking?" he demanded.

"Just an itty-bitty glass of champagne, boss. Not to worry," she mocked.

"I do worry," he said beneath his breath. He studied her face quietly as the music flowed around them. "Wade isn't the marrying kind, and you are."

"What difference does that make?" she asked, shrugging. "You know yourself that men only sleep with the carpenter's daughter, they don't marry her...."

"Eleanor, hush!" he hissed, glancing around to make sure no one had heard her.

"Why?" she asked. "Are you worried that someone might suspect you of playing around with the hired help?" she whispered conspiratorially. "God forbid!"

"Eleanor...!"

"I never knew until then that I had so much in common with the downstairs maid. Isn't that whom the master of the house usually seduces?" she asked, wide-eyed.

"Oh, for God's sake!" he burst out in helpless frustration. "Can't we have a normal conversation without sex coming into it?"

"Look who's talking!" she returned, stopping in the middle of the dance floor. "And I don't want to have any normal conversations with you. You're the only man I know who could probably talk a woman pregnant!"

He chuckled softly as he gazed at her, his eyes so warm they took the chill of the room off her. "We could try that, I suppose. How about coming with me on a picnic tomorrow?"

The invitation shocked her, but she kept it from showing. So he was trying to help history repeat itself, was he? Well, he wasn't manipulating her into any tight corners again.

She smiled and shook her head. "Thanks, but Wade and I are going sailing tomorrow. He has a sailboat."

The hand holding hers contracted. "He's on the make, you little fool; can't you see it? He doesn't give a damn for you or your feelings. He only wants to get you into bed!"

"Just like you did?" she probed.

He glared back at her. "You're not in his class," he began.

Her eyes widened and she smiled coldly. "Thanks a lot for reminding me. I'm not in yours, either, though, am I? Isn't it beneath you, asking the carpenter's daughter on picnics?"

He looked suddenly dangerous, those blue eyes glittering down at her through narrowed lids. Sensing explosions, she pulled out of his arms, regardless of the puzzled glances it brought, and went back to Wade as fast as she could walk. He was waiting, a faint smile on his dark face.

"Have a problem?" he asked amusedly, glancing past her to a glowering, blazing Keegan Taber.

"Not anymore, thanks," she replied. She smiled up at him dazzlingly. "Would you like to dance with me?"

"Honey chile, I'd love to," he drawled, and drew her lazily into his arms. "But do you think it's quite safe?" he added, nodding toward Keegan.

"Mr. Taber and I just had a minor difference of opinion," she said sweetly.

"It looks like he just got punched in the ego to me," Wade said conversationally. "You really don't like him, do you?"

"I like flies better than I like him," she muttered, glaring at Keegan. "Conceited ape!"

Keegan must have read her lips, because he turned suddenly and went back to the Irish girl, appropriating her from her current partner with noticeable flair.

"Just look at him," Eleanor glowered, "taking women away from other men, making passes at everything in skirts...."

"He's quite popular with the ladies," Wade observed. "I'm surprised you're able to resist his charm so easily."

If only he knew! "I've known him for years," she said shortly. "He's always around the house these days, talking to my father."

"And playing chess?" Wade ventured. He cocked his head and studied her while they danced. "Does

he really come to play chess, or to chance his arm
with you?''

''He'd get his arm broken for him if he tried to put
it around me,'' she returned curtly. ''And can we talk
about something else? You're ruining my appetite.''

''Oh, gladly,'' he murmured, and whirled her
around the floor with a smug expression that wasn't
lost on the tall, handsome redhead with the stun-
ning brunette in his arms.

Four

Wade kept his sailboat in a slip at the marina on Cave Run Lake. It was a beautiful area, in the Daniel Boone National Forest, and there were hiking trails and a skylift in the forest area. It was late spring, almost summer, and the woods were filled with picnickers and fishermen and hikers. Eleanor stared after them a little wistfully as Wade led the way to his slip at the sprawling marina. She liked boats but knew little about them. Her tastes leaned much more toward fishing and walking in the woods than toward water sports. It was another of the big differences between Wade's life-style and her own, but perhaps she could adjust.

He looked handsome in his white slacks and navy pullover shirt, not a bad-looking man at all. She glanced ruefully at her jeans and multicolored knit shirt. She hoped she was properly dressed for sailing. She'd remembered the tennis shoes he told her to wear, but he hadn't specified what kind of clothes to wear. She sincerely hoped he didn't have any ideas about taking her to an exclusive restaurant dressed like this.

"We have a budding sailing fraternity here," he was telling her, glancing over his shoulder with a smile. "In October we have the Grand Annual Regatta. You'll have to come with me this year," he added, taking it for granted that theirs was going to be a long-term relationship. Eleanor beamed.

"Is it all sailing?" she asked innocently.

"Mostly," he replied. "It's the first weekend in October, and starts out with around-the-course racing the first day, with a big dinner that night and another race the second day. There's an open regatta for all classes."

"Do a lot of people from Lexington race in it?" she asked.

He grinned at her. "Darling, it's only a short drive from the city. Even shorter from where we live, outside the city. In fact, the Tabers have a slip here, and Keegan and Gene won their class in the regatta last October."

Her face colored. She knew that Keegan loved sailing, but she hadn't remembered that he kept his sailboat here, or that his father raced with him. It was the kind of thing that Gene Taber would do, though. Like his son, he had a reckless streak. It was one of the first things she'd admired about Keegan, that recklessness.

"Speak of the devil," Wade muttered, staring past her just as they reached his slip.

She half turned and found Keegan Taber walking casually along the marina, as if he spent every day there and was right at home.

"Hello, Wade!" he called with a friendly wave. "You have a call at the desk. I told them I'd relay it, since I was on my way to my own slip."

Wade sighed. "I might have known. You can't ever get away from work, not as long as there are telephones anywhere on the planet."

"Wait until the cellular phones catch on," Keegan said with a grin.

"God forbid! Be right back, darling. Thanks, Keegan."

"Sure." Keegan stuck his hands in his pockets. "I'll watch out for Eleanor until you get back."

Eleanor glared at Keegan as Wade disappeared into the marina office. He looked as casual as she did, in jeans and a yellow knit shirt, and in deck shoes he didn't tower over her as much as usual. The boots he wore around the farm gave him even more height. The wind was blowing his red hair around, disrupting its slightly wavy perfection, and against his deep tan the white flash of his teeth was even more attractive. The wind was behind him, blowing the heady scent of his after-shave into her nostrils, drowning her in its masculine lure.

"What are you doing here?" she asked.

"The same as you. Enjoying myself."

"Aren't you a little far from home and your houseguest?"

His eyebrows lifted. "Which houseguest?"

"The one with the figure," she returned, smiling coolly.

"The one with the figure is on a tour of local farms with my father and her father," he replied.

"And you didn't want to go, too?"

His blue eyes twinkled at her. "I work hard enough during the week that I like having Sundays off." He chuckled.

She lowered her eyes to his throat, where fine red hairs peeked out. She remembered that his chest was covered with that softly abrasive hair, and her face colored because of the intimacy that memory involved. She wrapped her arms around herself protectively and stared toward the marina office.

"He won't save you, you know," he remarked. He pulled out a cigarette and lit it. "That sounded like his housekeeper Mildred to me. And she'd never bother him on a date unless it was an emergency."

"He won't go home," she said. "We're going sailing."

"Want to bet?"

She looked up at him, her eyes narrowed. "Not with a renegade like you," she replied. "You stack the deck."

He smiled, and little thrills raced through her body. She was still vulnerable, and she hated it. Four years should have given her some immunity. In fact, it had only fanned the flame, made her hungry for the sight of him.

Her eyes met his, and she felt her toes curling under at the pleasure of the exchange. The hand holding his cigarette froze in midair, and suddenly his smile was gone. She sensed his abrupt rigidity and felt it reflected in her own posture. At that moment she wanted nothing quite so desperately as to reach up and kiss that warm, hard mouth.

"Dangerous, baby, looking at me like that in public," Keegan said in a tone she'd never heard him use. He smiled faintly, but it did nothing to disguise the flare of hunger in his eyes.

Before she could answer him, and while she was still trying to get her heart to stop racing, Wade rejoined them. He was frowning, his mind already on business.

"I'm sorry as hell, but I've got a European businessman sitting on my front porch drinking my best bourbon and just dying to give me gobs of money for a foal." He sighed. He grinned at Eleanor and Keegan, ignoring the tension. "I'm sorry, darling, but I'm so mercenary..."

She burst out laughing. "It's all right. If you'll drop me off..."

"I'll let her ride home with me," Keegan interrupted, lifting the cigarette to his lips. "Then you won't have to go out of your way."

Wade and Eleanor both started to protest, but they weren't as quick as Keegan. He took Eleanor firmly by the arm.

"Come on, I have to pick up some papers from the boat first. See you, Wade!"

Wade faltered. "Well...Eleanor, I'll call you tonight!"

"Yes...do!" she called over her shoulder, half running to keep up with Keegan's long strides. She scowled up at him as he propelled her down the marina. "No wonder you have your own boat; you're a pirate! You can't just appropriate unwilling passengers!"

"You're willing," he replied without looking at her. "At least you will be when I show you what I've got in the boat."

She sighed. "Does it bite?"

"It used to," he murmured, grinning. He helped her onto the polished deck of the big sailboat, its huge sails neatly wrapped and tied, and went below for a minute. He was back almost before she missed him, with a picnic basket in hand.

"How...what...?" she stammered.

"I had Mary June pack it this morning for us," he said. He helped her back off the boat. "We can drive down to the picnic area and gorge ourselves. I didn't have breakfast. I'm starving."

Her mind was whirling. "You couldn't have known Wade was going to have company."

"Sure I did. I sent it over, as a matter of fact," he said imperturbably, herding her right along.

Her jaw dropped. "Your Irish guests!"

"Dead straight," he agreed, grinning broadly. "And he'd better hurry home, too, or O'Clancy will have persuaded Mildred to go home with him to Ireland. That man could get funding from Congress for a fruitfly-mating program. I've never seen the beat."

"You set me up!" she groaned.

"It's your own fault," he replied. He led her to his bright-red Porsche and put her in on the passenger side. "You wouldn't come with me when I invited you."

"I didn't want to! I still don't!"

He got in beside her and, flashing a dazzling smile, started up the little convertible. "Mary June's got roast beef and potato salad and homemade yeast rolls in the basket," he coaxed. "And she made fried apple pies for dessert."

She glanced at him mutinously. "I'll get fat."

"Is there hope?" he asked wide-eyed. "You've lost ten pounds since you came back home, and you were never heavy to start with."

"I like me the way I am," she fired back.

"I'll like you better twenty pounds heavier," he replied. "There. That looks like a nice, private spot." He pulled into a parking space in the deserted picnic area and cut off the engine. "Nice view. No people." He stared at her musingly. "You could make love to me if you wanted to."

The unexpected remark made her grow hot all over. She practically dived out of the car, avoiding his eyes.

He brought the picnic basket and bypassed the tables. "This looks good," he remarked, scanning the area. He put the basket down under a huge oak tree overlooking the lake. Far away, the white and multicolored sails spread like tiny map indicators over the blue, blue water. "We can eat and watch the competition all at once."

She sat down reluctantly in the pleasant shade, watching him spread the cloth and lay out the food. It did look delicious, and she knew Mary June's reputation as a cook. She and her father had been invited to barbecues and other special events that the Tabers hosted annually for their employees on the farm, and she'd tasted the housekeeper's cooking many times. Mary June was something of a family institution. Like her father, a treasured employee. The thought made her feel bitter, and she sighed, staring down at her hands in her lap.

"Don't curdle the dessert by glaring at it," he teased. "Eat something!"

He handed her a plate and busied himself pouring sweetened iced tea into plastic glasses from a huge jug that contained crushed ice.

She held out her hand for it and sipped the cool liquid with a dreamy smile. "How delicious!"

"I'm partial to it myself." He filled a plate for her, handing it over and ignoring her dubious expression as he filled another for himself. "Nothing like a picnic to make you hungry, I always say. Eat, for God's sake, Eleanor!"

Her dark eyes pinned him. "Must you always sling out orders? Can't you ever just ask?"

"Not my nature," he said between bites of beef. He sipped tea and watched her for a minute as she began to eat.

"No, that's true," she said after she cleared her plate. "You're a born manipulator. You're only happy when you get your own way."

"Aren't most people?" he asked. He put the plates aside and refilled her glass and his own with iced tea. Then he sprawled back comfortably against the huge tree trunk and crossed his long legs with a sigh. He looked as at ease here as he did at a formal party. Keegan never put on airs or lorded it over anyone. He seemed at home anywhere.

Eleanor sipped her tea, looking out over the lake. "I've never been here before," she remarked. "Dad and I drove past it on our way to see one of my great-aunts once, but we never stopped. We always go fishing on the river."

"There's a lot of bass and crappie in this lake," he replied, smiling. "So you like to fish, do you?"

"Dad does. I go along for the ride, and the peace and quiet. You don't get much of that in a hospital."

"What made you choose nursing?" he asked unexpectedly.

She held the cool, frosty cup in both hands and smiled faintly. "Oh, I don't know. I guess I always liked patching people up when they were hurt. I still do. I feel as if I'm giving something back to the world, paying my way as I go."

"Is that a dig at me?" he asked conversationally, but his blue eyes were serious.

"You work every bit as hard as I do," she said honestly. "I didn't mean it as an insult. I was explaining my own philosophy, not condemning your life-style."

His broad chest rose and fell heavily. "Maybe I feel like condemning it," he said broodingly. He ran a lean finger around the rim of his glass absently, watching its path. "My father built the farm up from bankruptcy when he was a young man. He worked hard all his life so that he'd have something to pass on to me, so that I wouldn't have to break my back for a living. Well, I didn't have to work, and it affected me. In consequence, I spent the first twenty-five years of my own life giving my father hell and expecting something for nothing. No matter how well meant, you can give a child too much." He looked up into her eyes. "I won't make that mistake with my sons."

"Sons?" she echoed. "Do you already have names picked out for them, too?"

"Sure," he said, grinning as the atmosphere changed between them. "Well, for the tenth one, anyway. I'll call him Quits."

She smiled, radiant. How odd, to sit and talk, really talk, to him. That was a first. She didn't want to enjoy it, but she couldn't help herself.

"How about you?" he asked with apparent carelessness. "Do you want kids?"

"Of course," she said. "I'd like a daughter, though."

"A daughter wouldn't be bad, although boys run in my family. The father determines sex, you know."

"No!" she asked in mock astonishment. "And here I thought the cabbage fairy did all that!"

"Stop it, you idiot," he muttered, chuckling. "I keep forgetting you went through nurse's training. I expect you know more than I do about reproduction."

"About some of it, maybe," she said tightly. She finished her tea and got up to put her cup and the plates in a nearby garbage can. When she came back, Keegan hadn't moved. He was still watching her, his eyes narrow and calculating.

"How about putting my cup in there, too?" He drained it and handed it to her, but just as she reached down to take it, he caught her wrist and propelled her into his hard body, cushioning the impact with his arms.

"Keegan!" she protested, struggling.

He only held her closer, positioning her across his legs, with her head captured in the crook of his elbow. He looked down at her, watching her struggles, feeling the touch of her hands on his chest as she pushed at it, and the blood rushed like lava through his veins.

"I'm not . . . on the menu," she said, panting.

"You should be," he murmured. His blue eyes scanned her delicate features, her full mouth and big brown eyes in a frame of blondish-brown hair. "I like what you've done to your hair, Eleanor. I like the new makeup, too."

She hadn't thought he'd even noticed it. Her eyes, steady and curious on his hardening face, reflected her puzzlement.

"You were sixteen the first time I kissed you," he said abruptly, watching her mouth. "It was at the annual Christmas party, up at Flintlock, and you stood under the mistletoe with the damnedest lost look on your face. I bent and kissed you, so gently, and you went beet red and ran away."

"I wasn't expecting it," she muttered, renewing her struggles.

He felt his body going rigid, and he stilled her with a firm hand on her hip. "No," he said softly. "Lie still. You're hurting me."

She froze, because even as he said it she could feel it. Her eyes levered back up to his and were captured by the mixture of hunger and pain she read in them.

"I'm sorry," she said, lying quietly. "But if you'd just let me go..."

"I don't want to," he replied. His possessive gaze traveled boldly from her face to the soft curve of her breasts in the revealing knit shirt, to her slender waist and her long, elegant legs in their tight blue-jean casing. "I'm sorry I hurt you that night," he remarked in a deep, velvet-soft tone. "I'm even sorrier that I didn't make up for it. By then, the risk would have been no worse. I left you with scars, didn't I?"

"Enough...that I don't want any more of them! Will you let me go?" she said, panting.

His voice was tender, the slow movements of his hand on her hip maddening. "It must have gone against everything you believed in to give yourself to me. I wasn't thinking about your upbringing; I was so drunk on the taste and feel of you that I couldn't think. I remember the scent of your body, the sound of your voice in my ear whispering that you loved me...."

"Stop it!" she cried, hiding her red face against him. Her hands clenched into fists against his chest.

"Stop it, Keegan, for heaven's sake! I was a teenage girl with a furious crush, and you were an experienced man out to revenge yourself on the girl you really loved. That's all it was!"

"Are you sure?" He tilted her face up to his quiet, solemn eyes. "I'll admit that I'd had too much to drink and had fought with Lorraine, and you looked..." His mind went back to the way she'd looked in blue satin with her long hair curving around her shoulders and her full, lovely breasts provocatively displayed in the strapless gown. "You looked like Venus walking. I only meant to show you a good time, kiss you a little. But when you moaned and started kissing me back so hungrily, I forgot everything."

It had been explosive, she remembered, the bare touch of his mouth enough to trigger unexpected longings. She'd wanted it for so many years, hungered for it, ached to know his lovemaking, his possession. She'd had a few drinks of her own, and when he'd started undressing her, she'd gone wild at the touch of his skillful hands on her bare flesh.

He saw those memories in her eyes and felt his body going tense. The soft warmth and weight of her in his arms was making him ache. She smelled of gardenia, and his mind wouldn't let go of the picture it carried of her that night in the moonlit darkness, writhing under his touch while the car stereo played an exotic, sultry tune that could still bring his blood up four years later.

"Don't you dare touch me there!" she burst out as his fingers went down to her knit blouse and edged under it to the bottom of her bra.

But his hand kept moving, and she could feel his warm breath at her ear, whispering things she didn't hear. She struggled again, until his strength subdued her. The silence around them was tense, broken by bird songs, the lap of the water on the shore and the rustle of windblown leaves. Eleanor could hardly hear them above the beat of her heart. She could even hear his, and she marveled at the electricity they created together. It seemed even more potent than it had four years ago, perhaps because she was a woman now.

"Hush, Ellie," he whispered, ignoring the hand tugging at his wrist. "Shhhhh. Lie still for me...."

She had to bite her lip to keep from crying out. He had her wrapped up so tightly that she couldn't even squirm. She didn't want his hands on her; she couldn't bear the remembered pleasure of it. She moaned sharply, hating the vulnerability that he could hear now as he found the front clip of the garment and gently unhooked it. She could feel herself swelling, and he wasn't even touching her yet. His fingers rested on the clip as the bra parted in front and began to peel away.

He lifted his head, finding her eyes, paralyzing her with the sweet warmth of that possessive gaze, while his fingers tortured her with slow, expert movements.

"All I want is to touch you, stroke you a little," he said in a voice as lazy and sultry as a summer night.

"Don't!" she cried, biting her lip hard as his free hand began to move the bra away from soft flesh. "Please don't do this to me, Keegan!"

"Why are you so afraid of it?" he asked gently, searching her wild eyes. "You're a woman now, not a child. Four years older, wiser, experienced yourself. This is just an interlude. Share a little pleasure with me, Ellie. Let me bring back the memories."

"They were terrible memories," she reminded him on a caught breath. "You hurt me!"

"I know, baby," he said softly, and his eyes for an instant were haunted. He bent and brushed his mouth gently over her forehead. "Once, but never again, never. Lie still, baby, and let me touch you."

She wanted to stop him. To cry out, to protest. He'd hurt her pride so desperately, and he was only playing with her. But he was calling her "baby," just as he had on that night, and she remembered the feel of his hair-roughened chest against her taut breasts, the smooth, hard muscles of his bare legs against her own, the unexpected steely strength of his body as he held her down and overwhelmed her in the moonlit darkness....

How could she want this, after the way he'd hurt her? But she did; she wanted it, her body was gently arching, and his hand was tracing her rib cage, taunting her, teasing her. "Shhhh," he whispered again. The arm supporting her lifted her a little closer to his chest, turning her so that her hot face could fall against his neck.

She shuddered helplessly and raised her hands, tangling them gently in the slightly curly hair at the nape of his strong neck. She couldn't breathe properly, and she couldn't hide it. She moaned again, a breath of sound that barely reached his ear.

His cheek brushed against hers. His mouth touched her ear, her cheek, her nose. "Ellie," he whispered, and his lips found hers, probing them delicately apart, biting at them.

It was just like that night. Explosive. Blazing. Frightening, a brushfire that hardly needed its own spark to ignite.

"Keegan," she moaned against his lips, shaking all over. Her eyes opened, anguished, and found a matching torment in the blue depths.

"Nothing's changed," he whispered, his deep voice a little husky with emotion. "Touching you excites me so. This, with you, is as satisfying as lovemaking. You make such sweet noises when I do this...."

"This" was an achingly slow tracing around her breast until his fingers brushed the taut hardness and made it throb with pleasure. Her body jerked and she moaned against his mouth. He reveled in the trembling hunger he could feel in her. Lost, burning up with remembered passion, he opened his mouth and gently thrust his tongue into her mouth. It was surprising, the way she tensed, as if she weren't used to this kind of kissing. Surprising, and wildly arousing.

His hands teased her body until he felt her fingers at his wrist, pleading, guiding. Surges of pleasure shot through him like fire as his hand found her, so gently, and she froze in the tender embrace, her breath catching as he took the delicate weight and found the hardness with his thumb. She jerked at that brushing contact, shuddering with obvious pleasure.

"Do you like it like that?" he whispered. "Does it please you when I touch them this way? Or is it better like this?"

His thumb and forefinger contracted, and she arched back, groaning, abandoned. And he went crazy.

She felt her body being forced down against the hard ground, felt the weight of his body as he kissed her fiercely, and was powerless to stop him. She was caught in the power of what they were sharing, in the sweet, warm beauty of it. Her mouth felt bruised when he finally lifted his head, and her eyes opened lazily to look up at the passion-hard face of the man above her. "I'm going to look at you," he whispered, catching the hem of her blouse while she lay helpless under his body. "I'm going to get drunk on you, and then I'm going to eat you like candy."

She moaned, beyond pride, beyond protest, wanting the breeze on her bare skin, his eyes, his mouth there. She trembled a little as she felt her rib cage being stroked by his lean, strong hands and the wind.

His face was dark with passion, his eyes glittering with it, as he looked down at her body, his hands just the least bit unsteady. Her arms lifted above her head as he raised the hem of the blouse just to the lacy bottom of her bra. Then, as he started to bare her breasts to his eyes, the sound of an approaching automobile penetrated their passion-hazed cocoon.

Keegan froze, shuddering. "No!" he whispered in anguish. He glanced up. "Oh, God, go away!"

But the car, loaded with children and a dog with a tongue half the length of his body, pulled into a parking spot right beside the Porsche.

Keegan dragged his eyes from Eleanor's shaking body and got to his feet with a rough curse, ramming his hands in his pockets and actually shuddering with frustrated passion.

Eleanor dragged herself into a sitting position, shocked to find that she wasn't even very disheveled except that her bra was unclipped. She fastened it unobtrusively as the family talked merrily and slammed things around getting out of the car. Eleanor had a glimpse of Keegan's obviously aroused body before he turned away and walked down to the water's edge. With a shaky sigh, she began to get the picnic items together.

She lifted her head and managed a smile at the group of picnickers as they rushed past to a table a few hundred yards away. She'd had a narrow escape; now she wanted to go home and mentally flay herself for the way she'd given in. She wondered if she might be a nymphomaniac or something. She certainly seemed wanton with Keegan.

He came back minutes later, still pale and rigid. He lifted the basket for her and carried it up to the Porsche, sticking it in the trunk with little respect for its age.

He held the door for Eleanor with a face hard enough to make her uncomfortable. She knew a little more about men now than she had four years ago, and she didn't have to ask what was wrong with him.

As they drove back toward her home, he lit a cigarette and smoked it silently, his red hair blowing in the wind with the top down. Eleanor kept her silence, too, ashamed of her behavior, ashamed of letting him see that she was still vulnerable.

He pulled up in front of her house and cut the engine. "I didn't mean for that to happen," he said unexpectedly. He leaned back against his door, watching her with an expression that didn't quite register.

"You never did," she replied curtly. "Well, if you're expecting me to be available for fun and games, you can forget it. I had one dose of you, and one was enough. I'm over you."

His thin lips moved up slightly as he read the fear so plain in her big, dark eyes and controlled the automatic urge to retaliate. He stared down at his cigarette. "I came on too strong, I guess," he said quietly. "I expected you to be experienced by now, Ellie."

"And what makes you think I'm not?" she demanded.

He looked up into her eyes, and the expression in them caused her to flush. She opened the door and got out, so quickly that she almost fell.

She was almost to the house when he caught her up with his long, easy stride.

"I won't flatter myself by thinking that no other man measured up, if that's what caused the scarlet blush," he told her, turning her at the front door. "Did I leave such deep scars that you can't give yourself again, Ellie, is that what happened?"

"Now you are flattering yourself," she said tightly.

He touched her hair, hating the tiny flinch of her eyelids that told him how very vulnerable she was, how frightened. "Don't," he said softly, tenderly. "I don't think I could bear it if you pushed me away."

Her eyes widened, shocked as she searched the blue depths of his gaze.

"Can't you see how hard this is for me?" he asked quietly. "I know how badly I hurt you, what I did to your pride."

"And what are you trying to do now, make it up to me with a little light lovemaking between women?" she accused angrily. "No, thanks! You caught me off guard today; some old memories got in my way and I lost my head. But that won't happen twice, Keegan Taber. I'd rather throw myself at a shark than at you."

He forced himself to smile, as if it didn't matter. "Would you? The shark might take off a leg. The worst I could take is something you once gave me."

"Something I can never give again, thanks to you," she returned. Her dark eyes flashed as she dragged them away. "Dad likes you, so feel free to visit him whenever you like. But I'm not at home to you anymore."

"Suppose...I didn't rush you." He sounded oddly hesitant, even hopeful. He looked at his deck shoes, not at her. "Suppose we got to know each other again—"

"In whose bed, yours or mine?" she interrupted, her voice chill and distant.

He sighed impatiently, and the iron control faltered. "For God's sake, I'm not trying to seduce you!"

"What an interesting denial, after what happened by the lake!"

He inhaled and seemed to grow two inches. "You weren't fighting very damned hard!"

Her lower lip trembled, and he cursed himself inwardly for that blow to her pride. It was the worst thing he could have said, justified or not.

"Ellie . . ." he began.

"Never mind," she told him, reaching for the doorknob. "No, I wasn't fighting, you're very good at seduction. I should have tried to remember how good, shouldn't I? Just leave me alone, Keegan!"

She rushed into the house without another word, hurt and humiliated all over again. She was horrified at what she'd done. Stupid, she told herself. He was the kind of man to take advantage of any lapse. If she wasn't careful, she'd wind up back in the same shape she'd been four years ago. It was very likely he was pulling the same stunt again, this time with the pretty Irish girl as the prize. Well, he wasn't going to pull the wool over her eyes a second time, no, sir. This time she knew exactly what she was doing.

As long as she kept five feet away from him, she amended with a wistful sigh. Her body still tingled from his hands; she could taste him on her mouth.

She closed her eyes and tried to picture Wade. But the only man she saw in her mind had red hair and freckles, and he sat in the living room with her father for what seemed like forever until finally he gave up and left.

Five

Eleanor stayed in her room until she was sure Keegan had gone. She didn't want to see him again while her emotions were still in turmoil. Who would have thought she'd be so vulnerable with him after what he'd done to her four years ago? She hadn't realized that she'd be quite so easy to seduce, but now she was forewarned. It would be a cold day in hell before she let him get that close again. Just remembering it made her go hot. To make matters worse, she knew it would take days to get over what they'd done together.

What bothered her most was why he'd done it. He hadn't seemed quite in control at the last, as if he'd been as crazed by passion as she. Well, he wanted her—she knew that. He'd never made any secret of it, either. But it didn't make things any easier. The hardest thing to take was his accusation that she'd wanted it just as much as he had. That was true, but she didn't want him knowing it. She had to remember what had happened before, had to remember that she couldn't trust him. Otherwise, she was going to find herself in another big mess.

Finally Eleanor joined her father in the living room. She'd reapplied her makeup, and except for the slight swelling of her lips where Keegan's hungry mouth had bruised them, she looked quite normal.

But her father's keen eyes didn't miss the swollen mouth, and he had an unbearably smug look on his face as well.

"How is it that you left with Wade and came home with Keegan?" he asked.

She cleared her throat. "Actually, Keegan sent his Irish guests over to buy one of Wade's horses, and then kidnapped me before Wade could offer to drive me home. We went on a picnic."

"Kidnapped you, did he?" He grinned broadly. "A man after my own heart."

"Well, it was underhanded, all the same." She tried to sound indignant. "I was looking forward to going sailing with Wade."

"Keegan has a boat. I'll bet he'd take you sailing if you asked him."

"He'd love that," she grumbled, "having me beg him to take me places."

"I doubt you'd even have to ask," he said quietly. "Easy to see he's got a case on you. I think he always did."

Fathers, she thought fiercely, glaring down at him. "Cupid Whitman," she accused. "Where's your little bow and arrow?"

"You might give him a chance, before you wind up with that Wade fellow."

"I gave him a chance," she said coldly, "four years ago. And he got engaged to Lorraine, remember? He's not putting my neck in a guillotine twice in one lifetime, oh, no. I'm older and wiser now, and I won't be manipulated anymore by your chess-playing hero."

He lifted an eyebrow and stared pointedly at her lower lip. "Looks like that statement comes a bit late, doesn't it?" he remarked carelessly.

She started to speak, threw up her hands and left the room. What was the use in arguing? Keegan had a ready and waiting ally, right here in her own house. If only she could tell her father the whole truth, he might not be so eager to push her into Keegan's waiting arms. But that was a secret she'd have to keep.

At times like these, she wished her mother were alive. Geraldine Whitman was little more than a soft memory now, the accident that had taken her life just a nightmare. She'd been only ten when it happened, and her father had been her whole life in the years since. Eleanor wondered how it would have been to have someone to talk to. She had Darcy, of course, but a mother would have been different.

She didn't see Keegan again in the next few days, and she was grateful for the breather. She went to work and on Tuesday afternoon rushed home to get ready for her date with Wade.

Her father looked depressed when she returned to the living room; he was sitting huddled in his chair with a scowl on his face.

"What's your trouble?" she asked him mischievously.

"You've run off my chess partner," he grumbled, and her heart leaped at the reference to Keegan.

"He's gone away? Oh, goody!" she said gleefully.

He glared at her. "No, he hasn't gone away. He just can't come down for chess. He's taking that Irish girl to a party."

She couldn't camouflage the pain in her eyes fast enough, although she turned away quickly. "Is he?"

"If you'd warm toward him a little... For God's sake, girl, he's going to wind up with another one of those heartless, self-centered little idiots, and it will be all your fault!"

"On the contrary," she said, forcing a smile, "if that's the kind of woman he likes, nothing I do will reform him. Dad, I don't want Keegan. I'm sorry, you'll just have to accept it."

He looked as if he'd lost his last friend. "Yes, I suppose so. Well, have a good time." He glanced up, approving of her full blue-plaid skirt, pale-blue blouse and high heels. "You look very nice."

She curtsied. "Thank you. Can I bring you back anything?"

He shook his head with a sigh. "No, I'll watch a little television, I guess, and go to bed. Maybe I can get back to work next week. I'm sure tired of sitting around here like a stick of furniture."

She bent and kissed his bald head. "I can imagine. Have a nice evening, Dad. I won't be late."

"Have fun," he called as Wade's car drove up.

Wade helped her into the Mercedes with a flourish. He looked debonair in a navy-blue blazer and white slacks with a white shirt and ascot. With his natural darkness, the contrast gave him a rakish look.

"And here we are again." He grinned. "Sorry about Sunday, but I managed to sell O'Clancy two colts. Forgive me for stranding you with Keegan."

"You apologized Sunday night," she reminded him, "and I accepted. It wasn't so bad. He brought me home in one piece."

"Odd, him being at the marina on a Sunday," he said carelessly. "He doesn't usually go near the place except with his father. I suppose it was those papers he had to get."

She didn't mention that she hadn't seen him get any papers. She didn't want to remember what had happened Sunday at all.

"I missed you," she said with a mischievous smile.

"I missed you, too," he murmured dryly. "Not that the Irish girl wasn't a dish. Very, very nice. Pretty face, good manners . . . a little mercenary, but nobody's perfect."

"Dad's miffed at her for costing him his chess partner," she mentioned. "He said that Keegan's taking her out tonight."

"Lucky stiff," he said with feeling. He glanced sideways. "Not that you aren't a dish, darling. How do you feel about feverish affairs, by the way?"

He might have been kidding, but she didn't think so. And it was better to have it all out in the open, anyway. "I don't care for feverish affairs, in all honesty," she told him with a quiet smile. "I'm sorry, but I'm the product of a strict upbringing."

"No need to apologize," he said, and for once he dropped the façade of devil-may-care charm. "It's rather refreshing, in fact. I think I might enjoy really talking to a woman for a change. This playboy mask is wearing a bit thin, the older I get."

Suddenly he was another person, something besides the surface bubbling charm. He slowed down as they approached the restaurant. His dark eyes cut sideways and he smiled, but it was a different kind of smile. "Are you always so honest?"

"Most of the time." She sighed wearily. "I'm hoping to outgrow it eventually." She half turned in her seat when he stopped the car. "Why did you start taking me out, if a quick affair was what you had in mind? Surely you heard about me through the grapevine?"

"Sure. That was part of the appeal." He sighed and smiled, a genuine smile this time. "I guess the reverse is true as well. What did they say about me?"

She remembered what Keegan had said. "That you'd been caught doing it every way except hanging from a limb of a tree," she said flatly.

He burst out laughing. "Oh, that's good. That's really good." He took her hand in his and lifted it to his lips. "In fact, there is a bit of truth in that rumor. But a lot of my reputation is inflated. I'm not really the big, bad wolf."

"You're a nice man," she told him, and smiled back. "I like doing things with you."

"I like being with you, too," he said, then searched her dark eyes. "Suppose we give it a chance. I won't try to seduce you, if you won't try to seduce me. How's that for fair?"

She grinned up at him. "That's fair enough."

He kissed her fingertips and got out to open the door for her.

Dinner was exquisite. She ate things she could barely pronounce, and Wade introduced her to a white wine that convinced her "bouquet" could mean something besides flowers. He taught her how to pronounce the gourmet dishes they ate and seemed to enjoy tutoring her.

"I'm so backward," she grumbled as she stumbled over a name.

"No," he said, and meant it. "You're a refreshing change. I like you, Eleanor Whitman. You may take that as a compliment, because I don't like many people, male or female. I've learned in my life that most people are out for what they can get. And a rich man quickly becomes a target."

She'd heard Keegan say something similar, years before, about not knowing if he was liked for himself or what he could provide.

"I'd like you if you didn't have a dime," she told Wade. "You're pretty refreshing yourself. For someone who's filthy rich, that is," she said.

He smiled at her over his wineglass. "Having fun?"

"Yes. Are you?"

"Oh, this could definitely become a habit," he said, lifting the glass to his lips. "How about dessert?"

She smiled back. He had a nice face. Very dark. No freckles....

Just as that registered, Keegan walked through the door of the restaurant with the Irish girl on his arm, and Eleanor wanted to go through the floor.

Wade glanced up, chuckling. "I'll be damned. You'd think he was following us around, wouldn't you? Hey, Keegan!" he called.

Keegan spotted him with Eleanor and smiled easily, drawing the Irish girl along with him.

"Well, what a coincidence," Keegan said. "Wade, Eleanor, I'd like you to meet my houseguest, Maureen O'Clancy. Maureen, Wade Granger and Eleanor Whitman."

Wade rose, smiling as he took Maureen's dainty hand. "How lovely to see you again," he murmured with his most wicked smile as he lifted her hand to his lips.

"How nice to see you again, too," the Irish girl replied in her delicately accented tones. "We enjoyed our visit to your farm." Her blue eyes smiled at Wade, and then she seemed to notice Eleanor. "Haven't we met before?" she asked.

"At the Blakes' party," Keegan prompted.

"Ah, yes." Maureen made the connection and smiled cattily. "Your father is one of Keegan's carpenters, I believe?"

"How kind of you to remember," Eleanor returned without blinking. "Isn't it wonderful how democratic Lexington society is? I mean, letting the hired help attend social functions—"

"Let's sit down, Maureen," Keegan interrupted quickly, recognizing too easily the set of Eleanor's proud head and the tone of her voice. "Nice to see you both."

He all but dragged Maureen away whle Wade tried but failed to smother a grin. "Hellcat," Wade accused as he sat back down. "That was nasty."

"Do you really think so?" Eleanor asked, her bright eyes smiling at him. "Thank you!"

He shook his head. "I can see real possibilities in you, Eleanor," he mused. "You'd be the ideal wife for a businessman; you can hold your own with the cats."

"I came up hard," she told him. "You sprout claws or get buried. She's interesting, though," she added, glancing at the corner table where Keegan and Maureen were just being seated. "Imagine how many years of training it must have taken to get her nose at just that exalted angle...."

"Shame on you!" he chided. "Here, eat your trifle and let's go. I want to get home in time to play your father a game of chess."

She gaped at him as he pushed the delicate pudding in front of her.

"Well, he likes chess, doesn't he?" he asked innocently. "I'll even let him win," he added, rubbing his hands together.

"He beats Keegan," she volunteered. "And Keegan tries."

He whistled. "Keegan beats everybody."

"Not this time," she said under her breath, and glancing toward the corner table, she smiled through a wave of pain. Old times and old tactics, she thought. Keegan, playing women off against each other, and the Irish girl didn't even know it. Perhaps she didn't care, either. But Eleanor did. She felt as though Keegan had always belonged to her, and it was hard seeing him with someone else.

It was understandable that she might feel that way, she told herself. After all, Keegan had been her first man. She only wished that it didn't hurt quite so much. She didn't dare let him see that it bothered her, either. He already thought, with some good reason, that she was vulnerable to him. It wouldn't do to let him know exactly how vulnerable.

So when he looked up from the Irish girl's face and caught Eleanor's eyes, she actually raised her wineglass and inclined her head gracefully. Then she turned back to Wade with magnificent disdain.

"What was that all about?" he asked with a faint smile.

"That was a congratulatory toast," she replied innocently. "He's bagged another one."

He chuckled. "You make him sound like a head-hunter."

"Why not? His reputation's worse than yours," she replied.

He lifted both eyebrows. "Do you suppose he's ever done it suspended from a tree limb?"

She burst out laughing, almost choking on her wine. Across the room, a pair of deep blue eyes saw and darkened with an odd kind of pain. But Eleanor didn't see them.

Six

It was just past midnight when Wade took her home, and she was still a little shaken from trying to eat with Keegan watching her. Had he really gone there by coincidence, or had her father told him where Wade was taking her? She had to know.

"I had a great time," she told Wade as he cut the engine of the Mercedes at her front door. "Thanks for the meal."

"My pleasure," he said sincerely. He leaned toward her, giving her plenty of time to draw away.

But she didn't. She liked Wade. Tonight he'd been there when she'd needed a buffer against Keegan. She owed him this, if nothing more. She smiled against his warm mouth and closed her eyes.

It was pleasant kissing him. Not threatening or explosive as it was with Keegan. Keegan. She drew back against her will with a tiny sigh. What was the use in pretending? No one would ever move her as Keegan did. She couldn't hurt Wade by letting him believe she felt something that she truly didn't.

He touched her face and shrugged. Then he smiled, without anger. "You're a nice kid," he said. "Hang around with me, anyway. I'll teach you all kinds of useless information and leave you panting with my expertise as a local tour guide."

She burst out laughing. "You crazy man!"

His white teeth showed brilliantly against his dark tan as he returned the smile. "It beats sanity, from what I've seen." He took her hand and lifted it to his lips. "Just don't let the rabid redhead see that lost look in your eyes, darling," he cautioned solemnly, nodding when her eyelids flinched. "Oh, yes, you're very transparent sometimes, innocent lady. I don't think he noticed, but you'd be a basket case if he did. Keegan doesn't play around."

She knew that far better than he did. She straightened proudly. "You're wrong," she replied firmly. "I had a crush on him when I was eighteen, but I outgrew it. I don't feel that way anymore."

"Of course you don't," he said, humoring her. He leaned forward and brushed a kiss across her forehead. "Be careful, all the same. I wouldn't like to see him hurt you. I've gotten very fond of you, miss nurse."

"You're nice people," she murmured.

"I try, I try," he replied, dark eyes sparkling with humor. "We're having a garden party Saturday. You're invited. I'll pick you up about ten o'clock, and don't argue," he said when she opened her mouth. "Consider it private tuition," he added wickedly.

"And how will your family feel about having the Tabers' hired help to entertain?" she asked hesitantly.

He actually glowered at her. "For heaven's sake, don't start that. All you have to worry about is keeping your head while you fend off my mother and sister. My dad will be a pushover." He chuckled. "He likes pretty girls."

"Well—" she sighed "—if you're willing, I'm willing. I don't want to embarrass you, though, and I have a quick tongue."

"Do you?" he asked eagerly. "Show me!"

She hit him. "You stop that, you animal," she teased.

He stretched lazily, still smiling. "Well, it's too late for a game of chess with your father, so I guess I'll go home to my lonely bed and try to sleep." He glanced sideways at her as she reached for the door handle. "Sure you won't go home and share my pillow, Eleanor? You can use half my toothbrush, and I'll even share the cover with you."

"Thanks, but my father has this enormous shotgun...."

"I withdraw the invitation," he said hastily. "I'm allergic to shotgun blasts."

She leaned over and kissed his tanned cheek. "You're a lovely man. I wish I'd met you five years ago."

"Yes. So do I," he replied quietly. Then he winked. "Night, love. I'll see you Saturday morning. Ten sharp."

"Wait! What should I wear?"

"Something wispy and feminine."

She watched him drive off, wondering what would qualify as wispy. A cocktail dress? She grinned wickedly as she went into the house. A night-gown...?

Her father had already gone to bed. She had to wait until the next morning at breakfast to ask him if he'd told Keegan where she was going with Wade. So it came as a shock, when she got downstairs, to find Keegan sitting at the kitchen table with her father, drinking coffee.

"Well, it's about time," Keegan muttered, glaring at her. "This is a fine way to treat an injured man, making him go hungry while you sleep off your hot date!"

It was barely six in the morning. She was half-asleep and, worse, wearing her old worn green quilted robe with only a flimsy peekaboo nightie under it. Her hair was disheveled, and she had no makeup on.

"What injured man?" she demanded, glaring at Keegan. "And what are you doing here?"

"Your father," he reminded her. "Just look at the poor man. He's so weak from hunger he can hardly sit up at all."

Her father was enjoying himself, all wide grins and flushed pleasure, Cupid in the flesh. His daughter glared at him, too.

"Weak from hunger, my foot, and who appointed you his guardian?"

"Well, somebody has to protect him from his heartless offspring," Keegan returned doggedly. His blue eyes flowed over her like the warmth of the sun, and that arrogant smile tugged at his thin lips. "Do you always sleep like that?"

He of all people would have to ask that question. She blushed furiously and turned away to start cooking breakfast before anyone could see.

"Are you here to criticize or eat?" she demanded as she started frying bacon in the big iron skillet.

"Eat," Keegan replied. "I'm starving to death. Mary June turned her ankle and can't get up, and Maureen doesn't wake up until eleven o'clock."

"Well, where's your father?" she asked.

"He went to the Red Barn for breakfast," he replied.

"Really? I'm astonished that you didn't bring him with you," she muttered.

"I invited him." Keegan sighed. "But he didn't want to impose."

She could have thrown something at him. And her father just sat there sipping coffee, enjoying himself. Men!

"I like my eggs sunny-side up," Keegan remarked as she started to mix some in a bowl to scramble.

"Do you?" She gave him a sunny smile. "How nice." She went back to breaking eggs into the bowl.

"Is she always such a bear in the mornings?" he asked her father.

"Oh, not at all," Barnett replied. "She's disgustingly sunny as a rule."

"Then it must be me," the younger man said with a sigh. He stared at Eleanor quietly as she moved around pots and pans, smiling at her stiff back. He was wearing work clothes this morning—jeans and a chambray shirt that probably cost the earth, she thought irritably. It wasn't completely buttoned, and she wished he would at least cover up his chest so that she didn't get sidetracked while trying to make biscuits. The sight brought back some very disturbing memories.

"Biscuits," Keegan sighed, leaning his forearms on the table. "Nobody makes them like you do, Ellie."

"How would you know?" she demanded, glancing over her shoulder as she cut the biscuits and put them into a pan.

"I usually come over for coffee with your father," he said. "After you're gone, of course, but there are usually biscuits left over. I love the way you make them."

Disgusting, the way that pleased her. She bit back a smile. "I make sourdough biscuits," she said. She glanced at him. "Go ahead, make a comment."

"I wouldn't dare. At least, not until you take up the eggs." He grinned.

She turned back to her chores. Keegan and her father started talking, and she got busy setting the table and getting everything cooked.

When she was through, she put the food on the table and started to leave.

"Where are you going?" Keegan asked with his fork poised over the bacon platter.

"To . . . to get dressed," she faltered.

"It will be cold by then," her father chided. "Sit down, for heaven's sake; you're decently covered, after all."

"My thoughts exactly," Keegan seconded. "Sit, girl, you won't inflame me with passion. I have willpower."

She made the mistake of staring into his eyes at that instant, with the memory of that Sunday afternoon picnic in her face. The look she shared with him made her tingle all over, and thank heaven her father was buttering a biscuit. She averted her eyes and quickly sat down across from Keegan, her hands trembling as she tried to pour coffee from the carafe into thick white mugs.

"Here," Keegan said softly, putting his hand over hers to help her.

She looked up, and all the years fell away; it was painful for her, so painful to feel that way about him and know that he didn't share it, that he had nothing to give her.

His fingers caressed hers as he helped her steady the carafe, and his blue eyes searched her face. "Did you enjoy yourself last night?" he asked in a tone like velvet.

"The food was delicious," she returned. "Didn't you think so?"

"Yes." He didn't release her hand when she finished pouring. He let his eyes brush over it, then reluctantly he let her move away.

"How did Miss O'Clancy like it?" she forced herself to ask.

He shifted restlessly in his chair. "She found it a bit trying, I think," he replied. "She doesn't like French cuisine."

"Then why take her to a French restaurant?" she burst out, wide-eyed.

"She didn't tell me until it was too late," he replied.

She wanted to ask if he'd known that she and Wade were going to be there, but her courage failed her. She concentrated instead on eating her breakfast, leaving the conversation to the men, who seemed intent on discussing farm business anyway.

When they were through, she got up to clear the table and put the dishes in to soak until she dressed.

"I have to run," she remarked, drying her hands. "I go on duty at seven."

"Will the world end if you're a few minutes late?" Keegan grumbled, almost as if he didn't want her to leave.

"No, but my job might," she replied. "Unlike you, Mr. Taber, sir, I have to earn my living."

"Eleanor!" Barnett burst out, shocked.

"It's all right," Keegan soothed him. "Eleanor and I have been sparring for years. Haven't you noticed?"

"Yes," her father replied, and there was a world of meaning in the word.

Keegan sipped his coffee quietly. "Feel like going sailing with me Saturday?" he asked unexpectedly.

She gaped at him. "Me? My goodness, you're courting the angels these days, aren't you, being so good to the hired help!"

"Oh, Eleanor," her father groaned, burying his face in his hands.

"I like the hired help," Keegan shot back at her. "And will you please stop embarrassing your father?"

"He's my father after all; I can embarrass him if I want to!" she flared, dark eyes angry and cold.

"Will you come sailing or not?" he demanded.

"I don't like sailing."

"You were going with Wade!"

"I like Wade," she returned. "I'd rather go fishing or walking, if you want to know, but I was willing to go sailing with him because I like his company.

I do not like yours," she continued relentlessly, "and you know why!"

He stared at her unblinking while Barnett watched them curiously.

"Besides," she muttered, dropping her eyes, "Wade's already invited me to a garden party at his home Saturday."

"At his home?" he asked silkily.

She glared at him. "His mother and sister will be there, as well as a number of guests. And before you ask, no, he doesn't do it hanging from tree limbs because I asked him and he told me so!"

"Oh, God." Barnett covered his face again, shaking his head. "Where did I fail her?"

"Will you hush?" Eleanor said to her father, then slid her angry gaze back to Keegan. "See what you've done now?"

"How could you ask him a question like that?" he demanded. "You'll put ideas into his head!"

"Dad's?" she asked innocently.

"Wade's! As you damned well know!" Keegan looked furious. Even his face seemed red, like his hair. He stuck his hands on his lean hips and glared at her. "Did he try anything last night?"

"Did you?" she shot back.

He was looking more furious by the minute. "Listen, Eleanor, you're going to get in trouble if you keep hanging out with that playboy."

"Dad, why don't you tell him that you're my father and that he has no right to grill me like this?" Eleanor moaned.

Barnett grinned. "But he's doing such a good job, darling."

She threw up her hands. "I'm going to work!"

"Running away?" Keegan taunted.

"You bet!" she replied without turning. She continued on to her room to get into her nurse's uniform and put on her makeup.

But if she'd expected that Keegan would be gone when she returned to the kitchen, cap in hand, she was disappointed. He was still sitting there.

His blue eyes gazed approvingly at the neat fit of her crisp white uniform with its metal nameplate. "Nice," he said with a slow smile. "You do look like an angel of mercy, baby."

Did he have to use that particular endearment? It made her grind her teeth, and the blush that covered her cheeks certainly aroused her father's curiosity.

"I'll be late if I don't hurry," she muttered, bending to kiss her father's cheek. "See you later."

"Don't I get a kiss, too?" Keegan asked.

She glared at him. "I only kiss family."

"How about long-lost cousins?" he asked. "I'll run right out and have a family history done."

She stuck her tongue out at him. "Beast."

"Have a nice day, darling," Barnett told his daughter as she went out the door.

She returned that, without looking at Keegan, and made a dash for her car. He probably wouldn't have come after her, but she wasn't taking any chances.

It was a long day. She couldn't seem to finish anything. There was one emergency after another, and by quitting time she was a frazzled wreck. Wade called that night, and she was barely able to talk to him for plain weariness. The rest of the week was equally rushed. In a way it was a blessing, because she didn't have time to brood over Keegan, who'd missed his Thursday night chess game with her fa-

First
Class
Romance

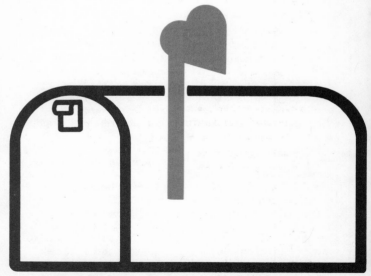

Delivered to your door by
Silhouette Desire®

(See inside for special FREE books and gift offer)

Find romance at your door with 4 FREE Silhouette Desire novels!

Now you can have the intense romances you crave without searching for them. You can receive Silhouette Desire novels each month to read in your own home. Silhouette Desire novels are modern love stories for readers who want to experience firsthand *all* the joyous and thrilling emotions of women who fall in love with a passion that knows no bound. You can share in the passion and joy of their love, every month, when you subscribe to Silhouette Desire.

By filling out and mailing the attached postage-paid order card, you'll receive FREE 4 new Silhouette Desire romances (a $9.00 value) plus a FREE Folding Umbrella and Mystery Gift. You'll also receive an extra bonus: our monthly Silhouette Books Newsletter.

Approximately every 4 weeks, we'll send you 6 more Silhouette Desire novels to examine FREE for 15 days. If you decide to keep them, you'll pay just $11.70 (a $13.50 value) with no charge for home delivery and at no risk! You'll also have the option of cancelling at any time. Just drop us a note. Your first 4 books, Folding Umbrella and Mystery Gift are yours to keep in any case.

Silhouette Desire®

A FREE *Folding Umbrella and Mystery Gift await you, too!*

CLIP AND MAIL THIS POSTPAID CARD TODAY!

NO POSTAGE
NECESSARY
IF MAILED
IN THE
UNITED STATES

BUSINESS REPLY MAIL
FIRST CLASS   PERMIT NO. 194   CLIFTON, N.J.

Postage will be paid by addressee

Silhouette Books
120 Brighton Road
P.O. Box 5084
Clifton, NJ 07015-9956

Mail this card today for
4 FREE BOOKS
(a $9.00 value)
and a Folding Umbrella and
Mystery Gift FREE!

Silhouette Desire ®

Silhouette Books, 120 Brighton Rd., P.O. Box 5084, Clifton, NJ 07015-9956

☐ YES! Please send me my four SILHOUETTE DESIRE novels FREE, along with my FREE Folding Umbrella and Mystery Gift, as explained in this insert. I understand that I am under no obligation to purchase any books.

NAME _____

(please print)

ADDRESS _____

CITY _____ STATE _____ ZIP _____

Terms and prices subject to change.
Your enrollment is subject to acceptance by Silhouette Books.

SILHOUETTE DESIRE is a registered trademark.

CMD4D6

ther because of some business meeting. Eleanor was looking forward to an uncluttered weekend.

Darcy went with her Friday afternoon to shop for a wispy something to wear to the garden party at Wade's home.

"This is getting to be a Saturday ritual," Darcy laughed as they walked through the huge store's dress department.

"Yes, I know." Eleanor sighed. "I just hope I don't run out of money before Wade runs out of places to take me. I'm not too keen on this garden party, you know. I won't even know the people."

"You're every bit as good as anyone else," Darcy reminded her gently. "Just keep that in mind."

"I try. If I didn't like Wade so much, I'd break it off. He's a lovely man, but it's never going to amount to anything serious. Bells don't ring."

"Bells are noisy," Darcy said firmly. "Settle for security. You can buy bells, for goodness' sake!"

Eleanor burst out laughing at her friend's down-to-earth practicality. "Oh, you doll, you." She sighed. "What in the world would I do without you?"

"Let's not try to find out. Now this is a nice little outfit," she said, steering her friend toward a heavenly little purple-and-white cotton frock with lots of ruffles. Sure enough, when Eleanor tried it on, it was perfect. It emphasized her long, pretty legs and her nicely tanned arms and face, and gave her the appearance of an ingenue.

"That's the very thing," Darcy said firmly. "Now, quick, get it to the cash register before you look at the price tag, okay?"

It was a good thing Eleanor did, because it was half a week's salary. But then she could always wear it to barbecues and coffees and other high-society occasions, like being introduced to the Queen if she ever came to Lexington.

She told Darcy that and watched the older woman's face crumble into laughter.

"You can wear it to church, can't you?" Darcy asked. "Besides, just imagine how many heads will turn when you walk out wearing that!"

Eleanor sighed. The only head that came to mind was a red one, and she tried to imagine having Keegan pass out with frustrated passion just by looking at her. That was some joke, and she just shook her head. No, by now the Irish girl probably had him halfway to the altar. That depressed her, so she invited Darcy into the nearest ice cream shop and treated them both to enormous banana splits.

Wade came by to pick her up at ten the next morning, and she felt so nervous that she almost backed out.

"It'll be all right," he assured her. "You look gorgeous, you silly woman, and I'll be right with you every minute. Okay?"

She gave in. "Okay. Just, please, don't strand me, will you?"

"I won't strand you," he promised. "Now, come on."

Her father had vanished earlier; she hadn't even seen him since she'd gotten up. She left him a note and allowed Wade to herd her out the door.

Wade's home was beautiful. It was almost as big as Flintlock, set in the middle of a wide stretch of pasture surrounded by white fences and racehorses.

One of the Granger stable had come in third at the Kentucky Derby last month, at the same time the Tabers' entry had finished second. There was great rivalry among stable owners, although Eleanor wasn't close enough to that society to encounter much of it.

"Like it?" Wade asked as he parked behind a Rolls in the driveway, near the huge brick house.

"It's lovely, especially the gardens," she replied, sighing.

"Wait until you see the backyard," he murmured dryly, and escorted her there.

Whatever she'd expected to see, the reality was a shock. There were tented pavilions everywhere, with ladies in wispy dresses and picture hats being escorted by nattily dressed gentlemen in ridiculously expensive leisure wear, with a huge Olympic-size swimming pool in the background. Everyone looked pleasant enough, and Eleanor's entrance didn't cause any riots. The guests didn't all rush together in panic and point fingers and speak in shocked whispers about the carpenter's daughter being included on the guest list.

"See?" Wade teased, taking her hand in his. "Now, they're just people, aren't they?"

"I guess so," she said hesitantly, her worried dark eyes glancing around. They came to a young dark-haired woman and a silver-haired matron, both exquisitely dressed, who were suddenly staring daggers at her. She sighed, expecting to do battle, because she knew whom they both favored. "Wade, would that be your mother and sister?" she added, nodding toward the hostile-looking pair.

He turned his head and grimaced. His hand, holding hers, contracted. "Oh, boy. Well, just ignore them, Eleanor," he said with an irritated expression. "They never like anyone I bring home, so don't take it personally. They're terrified that I'll get married and they'll lose control of the household."

"Let's go and meet them," she suggested, her eyes sparkling at the prospect of battle. "I love war movies, don't you?"

He laughed, surprised. "You little Amazon, you. All right, we'll get it over with."

She was dreading it, to tell the truth, but she wasn't about to spend the entire morning letting them make her uncomfortable. After all, the worst they could do was embarrass her, and maybe when they were through, they'd find someone else to victimize. During her four years of nursing, Eleanor had learned a lot about managing people. Buckling under, she knew, was a one-way road to misery. She hadn't let herself be walked on since she'd graduated from nurse's training, and she was now assistant floor nurse.

She smiled broadly at the two women, inwardly amused at the slight surprise that registered on their exquisitely made-up faces.

"This is your guest?" Mrs. Granger asked her son with a snooty look at Eleanor's dress. She lifted her chin. "Don't I know you, my dear?" she added with a faintly malicious smile while her daughter watched with a matching glint in her eyes. "You're the daughter of the Tabers' carpenter, I believe...."

"Why, that's right," Eleanor drawled. "You must be Wade's family," she gushed, reaching forward to drag his mother's white hand into her own and shaking it firmly. "How delightful to meet you both! I just can't tell you how astonished I was when Wade invited me. Imagine, little old me in a fancy place like this! I'll just do my dead level best not to slurp my coffee or wipe my mouth on my sleeve. Hot dang, is that a real swimming pool? You people must be just filthy rich!"

Mrs. Granger was openly gaping. So was her daughter. Wade was doubled over with laughter, no help whatsoever.

"I do love parties!" Eleanor continued, unabashed. "Say, is it okay if I strip off and go swimming in my undies? I didn't pack a bathing suit, you know."

Mrs. Granger cleared her throat and got a death grip on her glass of red punch. "I . . . uh . . ." she began, glancing irritably at her son. "Wade?"

He straightened, tears of amusement in his eyes. "Mother, you're out of your league with Eleanor," he said, wiping the tears away. "You've heard me speak of her—and please don't mind her atrocious manners," he added, tugging sharply on Eleanor's short hair. "She's had too much fresh air this morning, and it's affected her brain. Eleanor, darling, this is Mother and my sister, Sandra."

"I can apologize for my own atrocious manners, if you don't mind," Eleanor told him firmly. She nodded at the two women and smiled mischievously. "I'm very glad to meet you both. And you don't have to worry about having me cavort around the pool in my underwear. Actually, I don't swim at all."

Mrs. Granger was actually flapping, her face pale and her eyes startled. Her daughter was only a little less baffled and actually seemed to be amused.

"I'm glad to meet you, Eleanor Whitman," Sandra said with a grin. "Congratulations, you just passed the acid test. Right, mother hydrochloric?"

Eleanor laughed, delighted, and extended her own hand to meet Sandra's. "I'm sorry if I came on strong," she apologized. "It's been a wickedly long week, and it's telling on me, I'm afraid."

"Eleanor is a nurse, you know," Wade informed them proudly, drawing her close to his side. "She's an assistant floor nurse at Peterson Memorial."

"I'm impressed," Mrs. Granger said, and actually seemed to mean it. "Go away, Wade, and let me talk to Miss Whitman."

"No intimidation," he warned his mother. "I like this one."

"I never intimidate people," came the gruff, indignant reply. "Scat!"

Wade brushed a kiss against Eleanor's cheek and went off with his hands in his pockets to join a group of businessmen.

"Sit down, dear," said Mrs. Granger, guiding Eleanor to a shady umbrella near the pool. A waiter was just passing with glasses of ice-cold lemonade, and she appropriated three of them for herself and her companions, then sat heavily down in the shade, fanning her full face with her hand.

"It's so hot," she complained. "I wanted to be in St. Croix this week, but Sandra had to have help organizing this little social thing."

"So Mother always says." Sandra grinned. She looked very much like her brother and was about the same age, with dark eyes and very white teeth.

"St. Croix is in the Caribbean, isn't it?" Eleanor sighed as she sipped her lemonade. "We had a patient who'd just returned from there. It must be lovely, being able to travel."

"It gets boring after a time," Mrs. Granger said kindly. "Anything does. I enjoyed it much more when I was younger than I do now, although I confess I'm partial to the West Indies. The pace is much slower down there. I can relax."

"Are you going to marry Wade?" Sandra asked bluntly.

Eleanor smiled. "No."

"I see," Sandra murmured with a mischievous smile.

"No, I don't think you do," Eleanor replied. "I don't have wild affairs, even with fabulously wealthy men. I like your brother very much, but like is as far as it goes. I have a career in mind, not marriage."

"Well, I never." Mrs. Granger grimaced. "Just when we find a really suitable candidate, she turns out to be a career girl. What's wrong with my son? Isn't he good enough for you?" she demanded.

"He's wonderful," Eleanor said genuinely. "And I wish I'd met him years ago. But he deserves a woman who can love him to pieces, and I can't."

"It's all your fault," Sandra told her mother. "If you hadn't attacked her the minute she walked onto the property..."

Mrs. Granger actually blushed. "It's the kind of women he usually brings here," she confessed miserably. "And, well, there were some rumors about you a few years ago...." She blushed even more.

Eleanor had to bite her tongue to keep from responding defensively. "What kind of rumors?" she asked as politely as she could.

"About you and Keegan Taber," Sandra said quietly. "Lorraine was putting it around that you were the reason she broke her engagement to Keegan. She accused him of having an affair with you."

"But that's not true!" Eleanor exclaimed. And it wasn't. Yes, she'd been tricked into his bed, but one indiscretion hardly constituted an affair. "Keegan took me out one time to make her jealous. It worked; they got engaged the next day, and I left for nurse's training in Louisville that same week. That's all there was to it."

Mrs. Granger smiled sadly. "I'm very sorry. I don't know you, you see, or I wouldn't have believed the rumor. Mothers are very protective about their sons. Perhaps too protective in my case. Wade has very poor insight into character as a rule. Although," she added, "I'll be the first to admit that I have no quarrel with his choice this time." She offered Eleanor a platter of cheese appetizers. "Do have some. And wouldn't you really like to marry my son?"

"We'll arrange everything," Sandra added with a grin. "All you'll have to do is stand in church and say two words. We'll take care of the rest."

Eleanor laughed softly. Talk about wrong first impressions, she thought. Gradually, as the conversation eased to other topics, she got to know Wade's family. And what a delightful duo they were, nothing like they'd seemed at first. By the time Wade returned, she felt as if she'd known them for years.

"Is your scalp still in place, darling?" Wade teased Eleanor.

"Not a hair disturbed," she responded gaily. "These two are pretty nice, for rich people, that is," she added with a mischievous grin at the pair sitting with her.

"And she's not half bad—for a career girl, that is," Sandra declared. "We're trying to talk her into marrying you and taking you off our hands."

Wade actually flushed. "Now, see here...!" he began hotly.

"Oh, it's all right. I refused," Eleanor assured him. "You're perfectly safe."

"Whew!" He wiped a hand across his forehead. "And there I was, fearing for my freedom!" He smiled back at her. "Actually, I wouldn't mind marrying you, you know."

"Yes, you would. I snore and I can't bake cakes."

"You could hire a cook," Mrs. Granger interjected, shaking a finger at her son. "Don't take no for an answer, boy!"

"Yes, ma'am," he replied, helping Eleanor to her feet. "Now you've got to marry me," he told her. "Mother has spoken."

"Mother will be yelling shortly if we don't circulate," Sandra sighed, rising gracefully. "Can I bring you a fan, darling?" she asked her mother.

"Some ice would be lovely," came the reply. "Wade, introduce Eleanor to that Arab prince, she can't miss that!"

"Yes, dear."

"See you later," Eleanor called over her shoulder as Wade took her hand and guided her toward the punch bowl. "I like your mother and sister," she said after a minute.

"I'm glad, especially after the way Mother came on at first." He shuddered. "I could have dropped through the ground. She isn't a snob, you know, not really. She just . . ."

"She explained it to me," she replied quietly, cringing inwardly at the reason Mrs. Granger had given for her behavior. She'd never known about the rumors; her father had never said anything. Of course, he didn't travel in these circles, either. . . .

How terrible for Keegan, that his attempt to make Lorraine jealous should have ended in such a way. But why had she waited two months to break the engagement and then accuse Eleanor of having an affair with Keegan? That didn't make sense. Most of all, why didn't Keegan bear a grudge? He had good reason to, even though he'd started it all. Losing Lorraine must have hurt him deeply, especially since his date with Eleanor had apparently been the cause of his broken engagement. Poor Keegan. His manipulations had damaged two lives—his own as well as Eleanor's.

"She told you about the rumor, I gather," he said without looking at her.

Her eyes darted up to his set features. "You know?"

He looked down at her. "Yes. It was all over Lexington, thanks to Lorraine. She was rabid about losing him."

"But she broke the engagement," she faltered.

"Yes, that's what people think. But I know Keegan, and I knew Lorraine. And I promise you, she didn't do the casting off. He did."

That was a shock, but then, it had been a day for them. She bit her lower lip thoughtfully as they walked. "Why?"

He locked her fingers in his. "Maybe his conscience was bothering him, Eleanor," he said gently. "He treated you pretty shabbily."

She shifted in his grip. "You seem to know a lot about it."

"You don't remember, but I was at the Crescent Club the night Keegan took you there," he said. "I'd seen him in action before, and I saw the way you looked at him." He studied her fingers while she trembled inwardly. "At a guess, darling, I'd say he seduced you that night."

Her face went paper white, and when he saw it all the puzzle pieces fell into place.

He said something under his breath, and his dark eyes grew stormy. "So I guessed, did I? And it backfired, for all his manipulations. He got what he thought he wanted, only to find that Lorraine was as brittle as glass and just as cutting. She wanted his wealth, not him. Everyone knew, except Keegan. He was blinded by what he felt for her. But it didn't take him long to sort her out, and I'd bet it was what he did to you that opened his eyes. He never quite got over it. He's hardly even dated in the years since then. He has something of a reputation these days for leading a quiet life. The old playboy image is well and truly gone."

Keegan himself had mentioned something like that, but she'd only half heard him. She couldn't look at Wade. It was too embarrassing to have him guess what had happened.

He seemed to sense that. He touched her cheek lightly and coaxed her eyes up to his. "Don't worry. It's our secret. I'd never tell another soul."

She relaxed a little. "It was all over a long time ago," she said. "I have a few emotional scars, but I'm not carrying any torches."

"So you keep saying. But when you look at him, there's such a hunger in your eyes, Eleanor. You look at him as if you'd die to have him." He smiled gently. "And if he ever catches that look, darling, you're dead. Because he's doing some looking of his own."

"Conscience," she said tightly.

"Perhaps. Perhaps not." He pursed his lips, studying her flushed face. "Keegan's spent most of his life manipulating people. So suppose we manipulate him for a change?"

She stared at him blankly. "What?"

"Let's manipulate him. I'll take you in hand and teach you how to be a society belle. We'll go everywhere together, become what's known as 'an item.' We'll haunt his favorite restaurant, be seen at the marina, we'll do everything but announce future plans, and watch him sweat."

"He won't . . ." she began.

"I'll bet you a tuna fish casserole that he will," he returned.

"Tuna fish casserole?" She groaned. "Ugh! I hate them!"

"So do I, and the loser has to eat the horrible thing," he declared. "Is it a deal?"

She hesitated. "Why do you want to do this for me?"

"Because I like you, darling," he said gently, and smiled at her. "I'd love to marry you and take care of you all my life, but since you haven't a heart to offer me, I'll help you find what you want."

"And what do I want?" she mused.

"Oh, revenge," he said absently. "Maybe a little fulfillment. Whatever. Come on, Ellie. Let's give it a shot. Mother and Sandra will help. Look upon it as a project."

"Well . . ." She hesitated. It did have possibilities, however, and it could be fun. She smiled. "Okay."

"Good girl." He kissed her cheek. "Come and meet the Arab prince, and then we'll explore some of the more wearing social graces."

"Lead on," she said. "I'll follow." She only hoped she wasn't following him into quicksand. It might be fun to manipulate Keegan a little, but she didn't want to get caught in the middle. Once was enough.

Seven

We'll, well, look who's visiting," Wade chuckled as he pulled up in front of Eleanor's door late that afternoon.

Eleanor glanced at the red Porsche, a sinking feeling in her stomach. "Oh, for heaven's sake," she grumbled.

"And he wasn't interested, I believe you said?" he teased. "Funny, I'd call this hot pursuit, myself."

"Care to come in and have coffee?" she asked hopefully.

"I'd love to," he sighed, "but my dad is flying in from Greece. I have to meet him at the airport at five, which it almost is now. I'm sorry he didn't get to meet you. We hoped he'd make it home in time for the party."

"Some other time," she replied, and grimaced. "I don't want to go in there," she moaned.

"Chin up, girl," he said. "Remember—he's the victim this time, not you. Now get in there and tell him what a wonderful person I am, and how much you love my family, and how close I came to proposing! Lay it on thick. Spread it like butter."

She studied him. "Ever think of coaching a professional football team?" she asked.

"I sure have, but I'll settle for you right now. Come here, I see the curtains fluttering," he murmured with a grin. He pulled her close and kissed her warmly, smiling against her lips. "Nice." He laughed. "Like eating cotton candy. Now get in there and give him a taste of his own medicine."

"Yes, sir." She kissed him back, lightly, and got out of the car. "Do I look disheveled enough?"

"You look delicious," he said wistfully. "Oh, well, I'll go back to my cinders and ashes."

"Have you ever thought about having a glass boot made?" she asked. "You could give a party, and drop it...."

"I am leaving," he returned with mock indignation.

"A few white mice and a pumpkin might be a good idea, too," she added as he put the car in gear.

"I'll show you white mice and pumpkins, just wait," he threatened. He held up his hand. "Call you tomorrow."

"Good night. Thanks for inviting me, I enjoyed it."

"Me, too, honey. Bye!"

She watched him drive away, feeling wistful. He was such a nice man. It was too bad her heart belonged to that freckled redhead waiting in her house.

She turned, purse in hand, and went inside. Her father and Keegan were sitting in the living room, apparently just talking. Keegan was still wearing work clothes, and he looked as if he'd been out with his horses. He liked to work with the trainer occasionally, and in his younger days he'd participated in show jumping and polo. He was an expert rider.

"Hello, dear, how was the party?" Barnett asked, smiling as his daughter came into the room.

"Just lovely," she said with an exaggerated sigh. "I love Wade's mother and sister. They're so sweet."

Keegan cocked his unruly red head at her. "You do mean Gladys the gladiator and Sandra the snake?" he asked.

"Shame on you for calling them names," she chided. "They're terrific people."

Keegan leaned back against the seat. "Wade must have threatened to write his life story," he murmured. His deep blue eyes traveled over her slender body in the becoming white-and-purple dress. "I like that," he remarked. "The style is very becoming."

"Wade thought so, too," she said with a demure smile. "I'll get changed and start dinner, Dad." She glanced at Keegan. "Are you staying?"

"Are you inviting me?" he countered, his voice velvety and deep.

"You're the boss," she reminded him, watching his expression change. "I can hardly order you out of a house you own, can I?"

"Eleanor," Barnett groaned.

"Will you stop that?" Keegan growled.

"Okay. You're welcome to stay for dinner, Keegan, dear," she said with a faint smile. "I do hope you like broccoli and liver, because that's what I'm fixing."

"Darling, you know Keegan hates broccoli and liver," Barnett protested.

"I'm reforming," Keegan said through clenched teeth. "I love liver and broccoli."

Eleanor went down the hall to her room with revenge in her heart and a smile on her lips.

She changed into worn jeans and a loose patterned blouse that had seen better days. She didn't bother to brush her hair or fix her makeup, and she left her shoes off. That would show Keegan Taber that she didn't care what he thought of her appearance.

Bypassing the living room where the men were talking, she went straight to the kitchen and busied herself with getting the meal together. Odd, she thought, how much time Keegan seemed to be spending here lately. Whatever did he and her father find to talk about?

It only took about half an hour to get dinner ready. Eleanor called the men and poured tall glasses of iced tea for the three of them.

Keegan was quiet at the table, very reserved. But his blue eyes followed Eleanor as she moved around the kitchen between courses, pouring more tea, bringing dessert, moving serving dishes to the sink. His intent scrutiny began to wear on her nerves after a while, and she was glad when it was over and the men returned to the living room to play chess.

She washed the dishes, then slipped on an old pair of loafers to go walking behind the house. Their small yard overlooked the vast acreage of the farm, and from the wooden fence under the oak trees out back, she could watch silky racehorses prance around arrogantly in their paddocks. She loved to watch them move: they were so graceful, so much a part of her childhood. Like this house where she was born, where her mother and father had lived all her life. Like . . . Keegan.

She was barely aware of the footsteps behind her. She didn't turn, because she knew his steps as well as she knew her own. She didn't have to look to know that it was Keegan.

He came close behind her and stopped. "Why are you hiding out here?" he asked softly.

She shrugged, folding her arms over her breasts and smiling faintly. "Was I hiding?"

His heavy sigh was audible. He moved beside her, one hand tucked into his belt, the other holding a smoking cigarette. "It seems like it sometimes," he said absently.

"I thought you'd given that up." She nodded toward the cigarette.

He shrugged. "I keep trying." He lifted it to his thin lips. "How did you like the garden party?"

"It was very nice," she said. "Lots of people and food and even a band."

"Gladys likes to give parties," he said. He studied her body in the floppy ensemble. "Is that for my benefit?" he asked quietly.

"My ensemble?" she asked innocently, spreading her arms. "Actually, I thought it might inflame your passion . . . Keegan!"

He caught her with one lean arm, jerking her against the length of his hard body so quickly that she couldn't dodge in time.

"You inflame me all right," he said curtly. He was so close that she could feel his breath on her lips as he bent toward her. "Shall I let you feel how much?"

"Will you stop!" she protested. Her heart was beating out of control; he had to be able to feel it as close as he was. Her breasts were crushed against his hard chest in the rough embrace.

"Make me believe you want me to stop, Eleanor," he said tautly. His eyes darkened as they searched hers. Around them, the sun sprinkled dark leaf patterns on the ground and the breeze ruffled her silky hair. A horse neighed somewhere nearby. And in all that normalcy was this—Keegan holding her with his arm and his eyes, and the rough beat of his heart keeping time with her own.

"I'm off the market; haven't you heard?" she asked belligerently.

"I heard," he replied. "I just don't believe it. Kiss me."

She averted her face as his descended, and his mouth followed hers. His free hand dropped the cigarette and came up to tangle in her hair and hold her face where he wanted it.

"Now, fight..." His voice muffled against her lips as he took her mouth with his in a kiss that made her body throb with helpless longing. He knew so well how to do this, how to awaken her deepest hungers.

She pushed against his chest, but he only tightened his arm.

"Don't fight me, baby," he whispered as he lifted his head slightly and teased her full lips. "What can I do to you here, with your father right inside the house, hmmm?"

"I don't want this," she whispered brokenly.

"Don't you?" His fingers moved to caress her breast, then pressed it gently so that he could feel the beating of her heart. "Your heart's going wild, little Ellie. Just like mine. Here. Feel."

He took her hand and slid it into the open front of his shirt, hearing her sudden intake of breath, feeling the clenching of her fingers against his flesh.

"Here." He spread her fingers and moved them into the thick thatch of reddish-blond hair, watching her face as he felt the slow, involuntary movements of her long fingers. His heart ached with its hard beating. She aroused him as no other woman ever had.

"Ellie," he breathed. He brushed his mouth over her forehead, trying to catch his breath while her hands made him shudder. She didn't quite know what to do, he realized, but even that hesitant touching made his knees weak.

After a moment she put both hands against his chest. The weakness was growing: she could hardly stand up, and she wanted very much to move her legs closer to his. But she knew what would happen if she did, and despite her doubts and suspicion, she didn't want to hurt him.

He felt so solid and muscular, his skin cool under her searching hands, the thick growth of hair tangling in her fingers. She remembered much too well how that hair had felt against her bare breasts the night he'd made love to her. The memories were so intimate that she could hardly bear them. Even now, his heart was shaking him with its beat, and she remembered that it had been like that the night he'd taken her out.

"Keegan . . ." she began to protest.

"Shhh," he whispered. His mouth moved tenderly across her eyebrows, her closed eyelids. "Don't think. Touch me some more."

He guided her hands down to his rib cage, his flat stomach. He shuddered a little as her hands caressed him there. But she hesitated as he tried to move them lower, until he put his mouth over hers again and probed delicately with his tongue.

"It's all right," he whispered. "It's all right, baby, don't be embarrassed...."

She let him move her hands again, and he shuddered, moaning as she touched him. Immediately she drew back, shocked at her own boldness, at his groan.

"I can't!" she exclaimed.

"All right," he murmured. He drew her completely into his arms and wrapped her up against him, letting her keep a discreet distance from his legs as he rocked her in his warm embrace. "You're still very innocent in some ways, little one. It's nothing to be ashamed of. I like you just the way you are."

"You mustn't do things like that," she said firmly. Her voice was trembling, which robbed the little speech of its force.

"Aren't you curious about my body?" he asked quietly. "I am about yours."

"You already know all there is to know," she said tautly.

"No. I know a little." He lifted his head and searched her shy, soft eyes. "I'd like to know you in passion, Ellie. I'd like to see you the way you saw me that night, burning up with fulfillment."

Her face colored and she tried to tear out of his arms, but still he held her.

"I cheated you that night," he said, searching her face. "I want to make it up to you."

"I won't sleep with you again," she said shortly.

His eyes were calculating, watchful. He framed her face in his lean hands and made her look into his eyes. "I want to make love to you. That isn't the same thing as sex."

"It is with you," she burst out. "You just want to get me under your thumb again, Keegan Taber. You don't really want me, you just don't want Wade to have me. You see, I know you now," she continued coldly. "I know how your mind works. And what you have to offer me, I don't want, is that clear enough? Now let me go!"

The fear was still there, behind the harsh words. He saw it, and hated it. He let her go because this wasn't accomplishing anything.

"I have work to do," she muttered, embarrassed. She turned and walked away. Later, she knew, she was going to be very angry with herself for this show of weakness. She could hardly bear the thought of having let him see it again. Why couldn't she fight him off? Didn't she have a single instinct for survival left in her body? She wondered if she was ever going to rid herself of the hopeless attraction she felt for him.

"Why won't you listen to me?" he called gruffly. "You always assume you know exactly what I'm feeling, what I want. But I can't begin to explain it to you, because you won't hear what I'm saying!"

She turned to glare at him. "If I listen, I'll just wind up in the same shape I was in four years ago," she replied. "I'm not stupid anymore, Keegan."

"No," he agreed, "just deaf and blind." Frustrated, he stuck his hands in his belt and drew in a deep, slow breath. "Well, you may be stubborn, honey, but so am I. And despite all those fine words about how you feel and how you don't feel, all I have to do is touch you and watch you melt."

Her face colored, but she didn't look away. "You have that effect on other women, I'm sure."

"I don't care how I affect other women. Only you." He let his eyes run over her slowly, absorbed. "Suppose we go off someplace alone and talk for a few hours? I'll tell you exactly how I feel."

Showing her exactly how he felt was more likely, and she knew it. She managed a smile, then shrugged. "Sorry, boss man. I have a great instinct for self-preservation. You just stand back and watch me exercise it!" She cast him a defiant glare, then turned and stormed back toward the house.

Watching her, Keegan felt as if the world had swallowed him up. It was always like this. He could only get close by forcing her to yield, and he disliked the tactic. But she didn't trust him. Perhaps she never would again, and he had only himself to blame. If only he could tell her how he regretted that night four years ago, how he'd cursed his own behavior. Lorraine had left a bitter taste in his mouth, all because of Eleanor, because she'd bewitched him with her innocent body and her ardent eagerness to do whatever he wanted of her.

Eleanor had loved him. That hurt most of all, that he'd been so careless of her young emotions and so callously indifferent to her feelings for him. Now he'd give anything to have her throw herself at him and whisper that she loved him. And now she never would. He'd robbed her of self-respect, of confidence. He'd paid for it in double measure, but he couldn't tell her that because she didn't care anymore. She was crazy about Wade, emotionally at least, and the pain of that knowledge cut deep inside him. All he could do was watch and hope that Wade didn't put a ring on her finger before he could win her back. If he could win her back.

He, who had always been bristling with confidence, suddenly had none. All he could do was play a waiting game. And even then, it might be too late.

He sighed and followed her into the house. Well, she still wanted him. That was something. And he hadn't expected her to capitulate without a fight. She had to save her pride; after all, she couldn't make it too easy for him. He smiled ruefully. He was just going to have to think up some way to cut Wade Granger out.

Blissfully unaware of the train of his thoughts, Eleanor stomped back into the kitchen and slammed dishes around angrily.

He came in behind her, closing the door gently.

She glared at him. "Don't you have something to do?"

"I'm going to play your father another game of chess in a few minutes," he said. "He's on the phone right now with old man Jenkins."

"Oh." So that was why she wasn't being deprived of Keegan's company.

"Why won't you come out with me?" he asked unexpectedly.

"You know very well why."

He pulled out a kitchen chair and straddled it, then lit another cigarette. "We talked last Sunday," he reminded her. "Really talked, I mean. I liked that."

She had, also, but being alone with him, talking and growing close, was too risky. She'd just had proof of her own vulnerability.

"You still want me, Ellie," he observed quietly. "Yes, I know, you don't like having me know that," he added when she jerked around to deny it. "But it's true. And I feel the same way."

"I won't have an affair with you," she said, turning to stare at him with dark eyes. She seemed to be making a life's work of telling this to men, she thought with a flash of humor.

"I'm glad. An affair isn't what I want," he replied.

"You're more in the mood for a one-night stand, I gather?" she asked, smiling coolly.

"If you want the truth . . ."

But before he could continue, her father ambled into the room, grinning from ear to ear.

"Old man Jenkins is finally willing to sell me that bench press I wanted for my woodworking shop," he said gleefully. "He's decided that his arthritis is just too bad to do that kind of work anymore. Now I can throw out that piece of junk I'm using and do some decent work."

"When can you pick it up? I'll drive you over," Keegan offered.

"You wouldn't mind?" asked Barnett. "Then can we go now, before the old goat changes his mind?"

"What a way to talk about your best friend," Eleanor chided.

He grinned at her. "Why not? You ought to hear what he called me when I won that bet on the World Series."

She threw up her hands. "I quit."

"Only after the tenth one," Keegan said as her father left. He grinned at her expression. "The tenth son, remember? We'll call him Quits."

She flushed as she met his level blue gaze. "We?"

He let his eyes run slowly down her body, and the faint smile on his lips made her uneasy. "My wife and I, of course," he said smoothly.

Wife?...Was the Irish girl getting to him? She searched his face, confused.

"I'll be back, so don't go off with Romeo," he told her.

"As if I care whether or not you'll be back," she replied defiantly, her gaze averted.

"I'll make you care, somehow," he said. When she glanced up, however, he was gone.

It only took the two men an hour to get the bench press and return home, and then they spent another hour or two in the workshop behind the house setting it up and working with it.

Eleanor hadn't known that Keegan liked woodworking, but she should have realized that he and her father couldn't talk about chess and work all the time. She went out to see the bench press and watched Keegan run up a table leg on the lathe with quick, precise movements of his deft hands. He was good at it.

He was good at anything, she thought. Except maybe one thing...and even then, it had been her body's response that had caused her discomfort. It would have been uncomfortable with any man, but her headlong ardor had probably caused Keegan to be less gentle than he intended. And he hadn't known that she was a virgin, either.

She didn't like remembering. Leaving the men to their work and their talk, she went back into the house, set a carafe of coffee on the warmer and a plate of wrapped cake slices on the table with a note, and went to bed. She couldn't take one more minute of Keegan tonight. She'd had enough.

Eight

Eleanor got up an hour earlier the next morning, even though sleep had been long in coming. Wade had called after she'd gone to bed. Her father had knocked on her door to tell her Wade was on the phone, but she hadn't wanted to see Keegan again, so she'd had him tell Wade to call her the next day. She'd hated to do it, but Keegan was getting to her.

She was making biscuits when the phone rang. Her father was still in bed, so she dusted off her hands and answered it.

"Eleanor?"

The voice was male and familiar, but she couldn't place it. "Yes?"

"This is Gene Taber," he replied, sounding a little frantic. "Eleanor, I hate to ask, but could you come up to the house? Something's wrong with Keegan...."

Her heart gave a sickening lurch. "What's the matter?" she asked, gripping the receiver tightly.

"Nausea, diarrhea . . . he's in a bad way."

She took a deep breath. Be calm. Above all, be calm. She was no use to him hysterical. "When did it start?"

"About three hours ago," he groaned. "I thought it would quit eventually, but it hasn't. He can't lift his head, and he's having damned bad stomach cramps. I tried to give him something for it, but he can't keep it in his stomach. What should I do?"

"Call an ambulance," she said immediately. "I'll come right up. See you in five minutes."

What good she could possibly do she wasn't sure, but she had to go. It could be anything from simple food poisoning to a rupturing appendix; only a doctor would know for sure.

She dressed in a feverish rush, telling herself that it would be all right, that Keegan wouldn't die. But she kept thinking back to the day before, to what she'd said to him, the way she'd avoided him, and she felt guilty. He couldn't help being himself; he was just a playboy. She shouldn't keep blaming him for the past. And now he was desperately ill. . . . She had to fight the tears. Keegan was indestructible. He was never sick. But for Gene to get upset, it had to be bad. Gene wasn't one to panic.

She got into her uniform and didn't stop to fix her face. Two minutes later she was pounding on her father's door.

"Keegan's sick," she said without preamble when he called for her to come in. "I'm on my way up to the house. I'll phone you later."

"Keegan?" He sat up. "What is it?"

"I don't know," she said, worry showing in her face. She ran down the hall and out to her car. Even as she cranked it, she was hoping the ambulance would be right behind her. Dehydration, whatever its cause, could be fatal.

When Eleanor drove up at Flintlock, the front lights were on. She rushed up the steps onto the long porch, and Gene met her at the door in his robe. Except for some graying hair and the lines in his face, he was very much like his son, redheaded and tall.

"The ambulance?" she asked.

"On its way. He's in his room."

He led the way upstairs, filling her in as best he could. "He cooked himself some chicken for lunch yesterday. Mary June's been laid up with an ankle; she's just now able to hobble around a bit. I don't know if the chicken could have done it...."

Eleanor added it all up in her mind. The incubation period would be just about right for salmonella. Especially if he'd laid the cooked chicken in the same plate where he'd had the raw chicken, something a man not used to cooking might do.

Gene led her into a huge room done in greens and whites with a king-size bed in which Keegan lay moaning, half-unconscious. She went to his side, shocked at his weakness and pallor. He didn't stir when she took his pulse. His eyes didn't open. And even as she put his wrist down, he was sick again.

There was a pan beside the bed, obviously put there by Gene, and a wet washcloth in a bowl on the table. She grabbed at the pan and got it under his mouth just in the nick of time. She mopped his brow with the cloth and soothed him until the bout was over, and then she eased him back onto the pillows.

He was very nearly unconscious. Probably half-dead of nausea, too, she thought pityingly. Poor, poor man. She touched his red hair with a tender hand, pushing it away from his pale brow. She couldn't remember a time in their turbulent relationship when he'd been helpless. She cradled his head in her hands and bit her lip to keep from crying. He was sick all right, and he was going to need some intravenous fluid and bed rest in a hospital at the very least.

"Will he be all right?" Gene asked nervously as he paced the floor.

"Yes," she said, smiling reassuringly. "Of course he will. But I'm pretty certain that they'll admit him. He'll need to be given fluids."

"What do you think it is?" he persisted.

"I don't know," Eleanor replied. She wasn't allowed to give medical opinions: it wasn't ethical. "Don't worry," she added gently, "we'll have him better before you know it. After all, he's a Taber, isn't he? Tough."

He managed a weak smile. "Yes. I suppose so. Where the hell is that ambu— Ah! There it is!"

The siren was unmistakable, and through the pale green curtains Eleanor could see the red flashing lights coming up the long, winding paved driveway.

"I'll run down and show them where to bring the stretcher," Gene volunteered. "Are you going with the ambulance?" he asked over his shoulder.

"Of course," she replied without thinking.

"Give me your car keys," he said, holding out his hand. "I'll drive your car to the hospital and meet you there."

She handed him the keys from her pocket without protest. It would have been unthinkable to refuse to ride with Keegan, she told herself in justification. She looked worriedly at Keegan's face as he groaned, and clenched her teeth. It bothered her, seeing him like this. Keegan was so vital, so full of life. She was just realizing that he wasn't invulnerable, that he was just a man after all. Her fingers touched the red, red hair and smoothed it back gently.

"It's all right," she whispered as he grimaced and moaned roughly. "It's all right, you'll be well in no time."

It seemed to take forever, though, for the paramedics to get upstairs with the stretcher. She stood back, giving them the vital signs as they loaded him on the stretcher and strapped him down. Fortunately they were both big men, because Keegan for all his slimness was no lightweight.

Eleanor said goodbye to Gene as she followed the stretcher toward the winding staircase.

"Whatever is all the racket?" Maureen O'Clancy groaned, opening her door. She stood stock-still when she saw Keegan on the stretcher. "Oh, my God! Is he dead?" she burst out, putting a hand to her mouth.

"No," Eleanor said. "Just very sick. We're taking him to the hospital."

"Poor, poor man," the Irish girl wailed. She was beautiful even without makeup, her black hair around her slender shoulders in a pale blue silk robe, her blue eyes wide and concerned. "Do take good care of him, now," she told Eleanor. "I'll be down directly to see him."

"I'm sure he'll appreciate that," Eleanor mumbled, dashing after the attendants. Behind her, she heard Maureen's father ask a question, which Maureen answered, but Eleanor didn't catch the words.

Gene opened the front door for them, frowning worriedly as they filed out. Eleanor stopped long enough to touch his shoulder reassuringly.

"It will be all right," she said firmly. "Don't wreck the car getting there, please."

"I'll be careful. Eleanor, he's all I've got," he blurted out, the blue eyes that were so like Keegan's narrowed on his son's pale, writhing body.

"I know. He'll be fine," she said gently, and forced a smile. Then she ran down the steps to climb in the back of the ambulance with Keegan. She took his hand in hers and held it every mile of the way to Peterson Memorial.

Dr. Stan Welder was on duty in the emergency room when they brought Keegan in. She filled him in on the background and stood quietly by as the duty nurse assisted. Dr. Welder did a thorough examination, ordered an antibiotic and fluids and asked Eleanor to take Gene Taber down to admissions as soon as he arrived.

"I'll go with him," Eleanor said. "I'm not on duty for another half hour."

Dr. Welder nodded, his bald head shining in the overhead light. "Friend of yours?" he asked, noting her own pallor and the lines of worry in her face.

"Yes," she said without hesitation. "Will he be all right?"

He nodded. "Salmonella, most likely," he added. "We'll know when we get a blood workup. We'll get him into a room and give him something to stop the dysentery and nausea, and build him back up with fluids. Send his father down to talk to me when he's through answering questions for Lettie."

Lettie was Leticia Balew, the night admissions nurse, a capable and dedicated technician, well liked by Eleanor and most of the other staff. It was a good hospital, with some excellent health-care professionals. Eleanor felt fortunate to work with them, and more grateful than ever now for their expertise. Keegan was still important to her; tonight had brought that fact home with a vengeance. She couldn't bear the thought of losing him.

Dr. Welder noticed her uncharacteristic hesitation. "He'll be all right. I promise," he added with a faint grin. "Now go find his father, will you?"

"Yes, Doctor," she said automatically.

She cast a last, lingering look at Keegan's still form and grimaced as she turned and went down the long hall. Gene Taber met her halfway, pale and looking as if he expected to hear the worst.

"Salmonella," she said, quoting the doctor. "They're giving him something to stop the nausea and dysentery. They'll keep him, I'm sure, until they get some fluids back into him. He'll be fine now."

"Can I see him?" he asked.

"Yes. First, though, we have to give Lettie some information," she added, drawing her arm through his. "Meanwhile, they'll draw blood for testing and get him into a room and settled. By the time you see him, he'll be much better."

He didn't argue, but he looked as if he wanted to. "I should have stopped him," he murmured as they walked. "I was going to go out and get us something to eat, but O'Clancy wanted to see some videotapes of my new colts, and Maureen doesn't cook, you know. Keegan had a terrible appetite. Mary June will be sick herself when she hears about this."

"Salmonella isn't a killer, if it's caught in time. And you did the right thing," she said. She smiled up at him. "Now, come on, nervous dad, and I'll give you some coffee while you answer all Lettie's questions, okay?"

"You're a nice girl," he said sincerely, smiling wearily at her. "I was scared to death when I called you. Thank you for coming."

"I like him, too," she confessed ruefully.

"Only like, Eleanor?" he asked delicately.

She turned down a hallway. "Here's Lettie's office," she said cheerfully, ignoring the question.

She introduced him to the elderly nurse, then went down to the canteen to get coffee from the machine. When she took it to him, she sat quietly by his side while he answered the necessary questions. By the time he finished, Keegan was installed in a private room and sleeping peacefully, an IV in one muscular arm and the night nurse buzzing around taking vitals when they entered.

"Thank goodness it's almost your shift," Vicky Tanner said, grinning at her coworker as she jotted down the information on Keegan's chart. "I've had two heart attacks on the floor in one night. The medical staff has really been working tonight."

"I can imagine," Eleanor said. "Emergency was bouncing when I came in. How is he now?" she asked, drawing the nurse to one side as Gene sat down in the chair by his son's bed.

"Vitals have picked up already," Vicky replied. "He'll do, but he's a very sick man. His father got him here just in time. He's badly dehydrated."

Eleanor nodded. "Well, I'd better get down to the office so that Mary can give her report and go home to bed. You, too," she said with a smile. She glanced at Keegan, her dark eyes more eloquent than she realized. "I'm glad Dr. Welder sent Keegan to my floor. He's sort of a friend of the family."

Vicky studied her. "Yes. Well, see you tomorrow."

"Have a nice day."

"I hope to sleep right through it, thanks." Vicky grinned.

Eleanor went to the bedside and touched Gene's shoulder even as she stared down at Keegan's sleeping face. He was still pale, but his color was a little better now, thank goodness. "I have to go on duty," she said. "He'll be all right, you know."

"Thank God." He sighed wearily and shook his head. "There's only been one time in his life that he's been really sick, when he was about ten years old and had a bad fall. Otherwise he's been healthy—so healthy that it made this doubly frightening."

"He'll sleep for a while now," she told him. "But you're welcome to stay. I'll check on you later."

He nodded. "Oh, here." He handed her the car keys.

"Thanks for bringing it," she said. "How will you get home?"

He grimaced. "The O'Clancys will be right along, I'm afraid," he said with distaste. "My houseguests are becoming fixtures. And the last thing he needs is Maureen cooing over him when he can hardly hold his head up."

"I'll send Nurse Wren down to run them off ten minutes after they get here," she said gleefully.

"Nurse Wren?"

"The name is not indicative of her nature, I'm afraid," Eleanor told him, and smiled. "She's fifty, hatchet-nosed, and the hospital is her life and her career."

"Poor O'Clancys," he said, and returned her smile.

She winked, glanced once more at Keegan and left him with his father.

It was late afternoon before Keegan regained consciousness. He looked pale and weak, and he could barely lift his head at all. His father had gone home only minutes before, and the O'Clancys had stayed barely ten minutes before Nurse Wren got hold of them. Eleanor almost felt guilty for sending Wren into the room, but it had bothered her—in unexpected ways—to see that Irish woman bending over Keegan so lovingly and kissing his helpless face. She did feel possessive about Keegan; she couldn't help it. She'd shared something with him that she'd never shared with anyone else, that she never wanted to share with anyone else. She hated the thought of that Maureen person touching him, being with him as she had. It was beyond bearing. Seeing Maureen kissing him triggered a horrible emptiness in her. She'd come face to face with reality, with the fact that she'd never really have Keegan. Not his love, or any kind of future with him. He'd marry someone like Maureen, and she would be alone, as she'd been alone since she'd left Lexington four years ago. Despite his desire for her, Keegan would never be able to give her what she wanted most: his love.

She had to force herself to walk to his bed, to take his temperature and pulse and blood pressure with cool professionalism. Especially with those very blue eyes wide open and watching every move she made.

"Out...of uniform," he said weakly, and tried to smile as she pumped up the cuff she'd fixed around his arm and read his blood pressure.

"What?" she asked.

"Your cap."

She sighed. "I left it at home," she replied. "Your father called as I was making breakfast. I barely took time to dress."

He caught her hand as she removed the instrument, holding her fingers despite her feeble effort to free them.

"Thank you," he said quietly.

"It's my job," she replied, and gently took his fingers from hers and put them back over his chest. "Rest now. You've been dreadfully sick."

"Told you...my own cooking would...kill me someday," he murmured drowsily.

"It very nearly did," she said quietly. She reached down and smoothed back his unruly hair. It was cool and damp under her fingers. "Get some rest now. You've had a rough night."

"My stomach is sore." He grimaced, touching it through the sheet.

"I guess so," she said, "with all those spasms. By tomorrow, you'll be much better."

"Stay with me," he whispered, clutching at her skirt.

That went through her like an arrow, that whispered plea. He was sedated and surely didn't know what he was saying; she realized that. But it was so sweet, thinking that he cared enough to want her with him.

She touched his hand with hers and held it until he fell asleep again. Then she tucked it back under the cover and pulled the sheet over him.

Sleep well, my darling, she thought tenderly. She had to force herself to go out the door and leave him. But he hadn't known what he was saying, of course. It was just the aftereffects of all he'd been through.

Gene was back just before three, as Eleanor was going off duty. She told him how Keegan was and mentioned that he was asleep. He said he'd wait until she gave her report and buy her a cup of coffee. She almost refused, but he looked so alone.

"Okay," she relented. "I'll be back in ten minutes. Meet you in the canteen."

Quickly she gave her report and went off duty. Gene was sitting at a table in the small canteen just beyond the waiting rooms.

"It's been a long day," he said with a smile.

"I can imagine." She stared into her coffee cup. "He's better, but still weak. But tomorrow he'll be screaming to get out of here. You wait and see."

"I'll enjoy hearing him scream, after this," he told her. He leaned back in his chair and studied her drawn face. "Still hurts, does it?" he asked levelly.

She lifted her chin. "I'm over all that," she declared.

"Bull," he replied pleasantly. "Not much, you aren't, judging by the way you came running this morning when I called you. You were as horrified as I was, professional training and all."

She smiled miserably. "I guess I was," she admitted. "He's a very special man."

"I think so. He's been spoiled rotten, of course," he told her with a rakish grin. "I'm not sorry, either.

I came up rough. I never had anything. So I made up for it with him. If his mother hadn't died giving birth to him, all that might have been different. But after I lost her, he became my whole world. I'd have done anything for him." He sipped coffee. "Women have done their share of spoiling, too, though."

"Yes." She sighed.

He studied her lowered face. "He used to talk about you all the time, after you left Lexington," he commented.

Her face lifted involuntarily, her dark eyes quiet and curious. "Did he?"

"I thought it odd at the time," he confessed, "especially in view of the fact that he'd only taken you out that one time. He was engaged to Lorraine, too. Yet you were the one he talked about."

She sighed. "I found out why he took me out. It was to bring Lorraine up to par, to make her accept his proposal. He manipulated both of us, and it worked."

"Did it? Oh, he got Lorraine all right. But once he had her, he couldn't get rid of her fast enough. He drove her away, Eleanor. He neglected her, ignored her, deliberately baited her until she broke off the engagement."

Her heart began to race. "I hurt his conscience," she said tightly. "He said so."

"He manipulated you both, but it backfired," he said. His blue eyes searched her face. "He cared about you. He really cared. It was a shame you left town when you did."

He couldn't know how that hurt. But she smiled in spite of the pain. "Think so?" she asked, toying with her coffee cup. "Perhaps it was just an attack of guilt."

"Who knows?" he said, watching her. "Don't let that Irish filly drag him off to the altar, Eleanor. She wants him, and he may decide he's got nothing else to hold him here."

"It would be a good match, though, don't you think?" she commented, even though it was killing her to admit it. "She's wealthy and well-bred, and she'd fit into his world very well."

"And you don't think you would?" he shot at her, blue eyes flashing. "Balderdash! I didn't raise my boy to be a snob, Eleanor, and neither am I. You're more than welcome in my home any time, in any way. And don't start throwing that line at me about just being the carpenter's daughter. It won't wash with me!"

"Ferocious old thing, aren't you?" She laughed.

"You bet, when it comes to social warfare." He finished his coffee. "I like you, girl. You've got style and a temper to match my son's."

"I like you, too," she replied. "I have to get home and feed Dad. You'll, uh, let me know if there's any change?" she added hesitantly.

He searched her concerned eyes. "Sure. Care to come back and sit with him tonight?"

She wanted to, desperately. But she shook her head. "You'll do him more good than I will," she said softly. "I'll see you in the morning. Take care. Of both of you."

He nodded. "Thanks again for all you've done."

"I've only done my job," she demurred. Smiling at him, she put the empty cup in the trash can and left.

It was a long night. She paced and paced, until her father mentioned that she might have a game of chess with him. That made it worse, reminded her of Keegan and happier times.

"Go see him, for God's sake, if you're that worried," Barnett suggested.

"I'm not worried!" she snapped.

He shook his head, grinning. "He's tough. He'll be all right. Gene said so. He came by earlier to tell me how Keegan was getting on. Said he didn't know which of the three of you looked worse when the ambulance got there. He was afraid you were going to flake out, too, when you saw Keegan."

"He looked pretty bad," she mumbled evasively.

"I imagine so. He'll probably never eat his own cooking again," he added dryly. "I'm glad the boy's all right. I'm rather fond of him."

So was Eleanor. All too fond. But she said nothing.

Keegan was sitting up in bed when she went on duty the next morning, still pale but bristling with impatience to get on his feet again.

"It's about time you showed up," he grumbled as she walked into the room. His blue eyes glared up at her. "I've been awakened from a sound sleep and forcibly bathed by some horrible old woman with cold hands, I've been poked and prodded by a doctor, someone came and took half my blood with a horrible long needle.... Where were you?"

She had to fight down laughter. "I've been at home sleeping, of course," she replied, going to the bed. "You look much better today. How do you feel?"

"Empty," he said shortly. "How about a steak? On second thought, how about a whole steer?"

She checked his chart and smiled. "Nope. Liquids and semisolids today. If that stays down all right, then we'll see about something more substantial."

"Conspiracy," he accused. "You and that doctor are in league together."

"Of course." She curtsied. "We're your professional health-care team. We have to take good care of you."

"You're starving me to death, that's what you're doing."

"Eating is what got you here in the first place," she reminded him. "Here." She stuck the thermometer in his mouth while she took his pulse. He looked up at her, at the neat fit of her white uniform. His piercing eyes paused on her breasts, and she felt his pulse jump as she took it.

By the time she got to his blood pressure, his watchful gaze was frankly disturbing. She was glad no one was taking her pulse!

She finished reading vitals and jotted them down on his chart.

"When do I get out of here?" he demanded.

"Not today," she said cheerfully. "How about something to read?"

He sighed in frustration. "Dad will bring the *Wall Street Journal* in when he comes."

She lifted an eyebrow. "Well, we do have a local daily paper in Lexington, you know."

"I know who did what," he told her. "The only reason people read the paper is to find out who got caught at it."

"Cynic," she accused.

"I've got more reason to be cynical than most," he responded. "God, you look sweet in that uniform," he added softly.

She avoided looking directly at him. "Would you like something to drink?" she asked.

"The ministering angel of mercy," he said with a smile. "Yes, it suits you. You always did care about people, even when you were a kid. You were forever patching up one of your playmates."

"How do you know that?"

"Your father. We talk about you a lot," he replied, folding his arms over his bare chest. The sheet had slid down around his lean waist, and she was almost sure he didn't have pajamas on under it.

"You're supposed to be wearing a hospital gown," she told him.

"What for?" he asked lazily. "I sleep raw at home, and this is a private room."

"We have candy stripers here," she said. "Young girls who don't exactly need the kind of education they'd get if they came in when you were on your way to the bathroom."

He raised an eyebrow, noticing the way she averted her eyes from his hair-covered chest and muscular stomach. "Do I bother you this way?"

"I went through four years of nurse's training." She looked directly at him. "And I have seen you without your clothes once, if you remember."

"Bravo, honey," he murmured gently. "Do you realize that's the first time you've ever brought the subject up by yourself?"

"As you said once, it was a long time ago," she replied.

"Not so long that I can forget it," he said quietly. He searched her dark eyes. "You haunt me."

"Hire an exorcist," she suggested, then checked her watch. "I have to run. We're overloaded with patients today. Mostly women." She grinned at him. "I imagine they've all come up with various ill-nesses just because they heard you were a patient."

He smiled, and it warmed her like sunshine. "Think so?" he asked.

"Oh, definitely."

"Do you have to go?" he asked as she paused at the door.

"Afraid so. I'm the assistant floor nurse these days. That means if the supervisor is missing, my head rolls in her place." She grinned.

He tilted his head. "Such a pretty head to meet such a horrible fate," he remarked. "Wouldn't you rather sit and hold my hand instead?"

"Miss O'Clancy will do that for you, I'm sure," she said with admirable indifference. "If you need anything, ring the buzzer."

"I need you," he said softly. "Will you come if I call?"

"Only in case of emergency." She laughed. "See you later."

It was an oddly satisfying day. She popped in and out of Keegan's room as time permitted, and he flirted outrageously with her. She ignored his pro-vocative remarks, though, and was completely professional in her behavior. He seemed puzzled as he watched her go about her duties, competent and secure in a position of responsibility. For once he was on the receiving end of the orders, and she saw him smile at the irony of their reversed positions.

"You're different here," he remarked just after his dinner had been served and Eleanor cleared the dishes away to take his vital signs again. "Very much the career girl. Do you enjoy it?"

"The responsibility gets heavy from time to time," she confessed. "But yes, I do enjoy it."

"You run all the time," he grumbled as she finished with him and tucked her pen back into her pocket.

"I have to," she said, smiling at him. "I have a lot of patients on this floor sicker than you are. There's a heart attack in 4B, and a bleeding ulcer in 4F, and I've got an appendectomy next door, pneumonia down the hall...."

"I get the general idea," he said dryly. "Come here."

Her heart leaped, but she managed a smile. "Why?"

"Because I asked you to," he replied.

"Sorry. We're not allowed to fraternize with the patients," she told him.

"I don't want to fraternize," he replied, and grinned wickedly. "I just want to drag you down here and let you take my pulse again."

The image made her smile. "Lecher," she scolded, shaking her head. "Behave yourself, or I'll send Nurse Wren after you."

He shuddered. "God forbid!"

"Then mind your manners," she ordered, backing toward the door, "or I'll...Oops!"

"Oh, excuse me," Maureen O'Clancy said sweetly as she opened the door right into Eleanor. "I'm sorry, nurse, I didn't see you!"

Nine

Forcing a smile to her lips was the hardest thing Eleanor had ever done. But she managed it.

"No harm done," she said sweetly. "If you'll excuse me, I'll get back to my paperwork."

"Amazing, that you can find time to visit the patients," Maureen said as sweetly, her blue eyes flashing.

"Visiting them is my job," Eleanor reminded her. "And despite the posted visiting hours, we don't like our patients to get too tired," she added in her best floor nurse's tone. "Good day."

"Well!..." Maureen said haughtily as the door closed.

Eleanor couldn't help smiling as she strode down the hall. There was something about that Irish girl....

"Phone call, love!" Darcy called to her from the desk. "It's your Mr. Granger, I think."

"Finally, a bright spot in my day," Eleanor laughed as she took the receiver from her friend's outstretched hand.

"I heard that," Wade drawled in her ear. "Have you missed me? I just heard about Keegan. How is he?"

"Reviving nicely, and at the moment being cuddled and cooed over by his Irish girlfriend," she replied carelessly.

"If I were in his place, I'd settle for you, pretty girl," he laughed. "How about dinner tonight? I'll take you out for spaghetti."

"I'd love it!" she said enthusiastically. "What time?"

"Pick you up at six."

"I'll look forward to it. Bye."

She hung up and hummed a tune as she dealt with supply sheets. Minutes later, Maureen O'Clancy marched past the desk with her nose looking definitely out of joint. She didn't even spare Eleanor a glance as she left the hospital.

"Well," Darcy huffed, "what was that all about?"

"I don't know. Uh-oh, looks like she upset our patient," Eleanor added, glancing at the board: Keegan's light was on. "I'd better go and see about him."

She found him lying back on his pillows looking grim, his arms folded defensively over his chest. He glanced up as she entered the room.

"What kept you?" he snapped at her. "I want my clothes. Now!"

"What brought this on?" she asked.

He sat up straighter. "That Irish bounder O'Clancy is about to talk my father out of Straightaway. For God's sake, he won the Preakness last year, I don't want him sold! And Dad's a sucker for a sob story. O'Clancy will have him charmed if I don't get home!"

"Why not phone your father and talk to him?" she suggested.

"That won't help," he said curtly. "Just get my clothes."

Eleanor leaned back against the door with a sigh. "Do be reasonable. You're just barely off the IV. You're too weak to be running around yet. Besides, are you sure it's the truth, about Maureen's father, I mean? Perhaps Maureen just wants you home again."

Saying that was a mistake. "Do you think so, honey?" he asked softly, his eyes cold and angry. "Maybe it'll be refreshing to have a woman want me for a change."

"Then by all means, we'll send you home as soon as Dr. Welder says we can release you," she replied acidly. "But for now... What are you doing?"

He was climbing out of bed, that's what he was doing, and without a stitch of clothing on his body. He faltered a little, then he straightened and went directly toward Eleanor.

She tried not to look. Arrow-straight body, hair-roughened chest and stomach and thighs, powerful long legs, powerful shoulders without the camouflage of clothing. He was beautiful.

He stopped just in front of her, breathing a little heavily from the exertion. "My clothes," he said quietly. "Or I'll walk out just the way I am."

Eleanor swallowed. "I don't have the authority to release you," she said.

He put his hands against the door on either side of her head and searched her soft dark eyes with his. "Every time I do this, you fight. Or you run. You won't even give me a chance, will you?"

"As you just observed, it might be refreshing to have a woman want you for a change," she said softly. "You might as well give Maureen a whirl, Keegan. She'd fit very well into your life."

Gently he fingered a strand of her honey-brown hair, testing its silkiness. "Snob," he murmured.

"I'm realistic," she corrected.

"Is that what you call it?" He hesitated, searching her eyes for a response. "Ellie, could we kiss each other just once without any coercion at all, do you think? Just for old times' sake?"

"I'm on duty," she protested weakly.

"You don't have anything to be afraid of," he said softly. "Not anything at all. Just close your eyes, little one, and let me do it all this time."

There were a thousand reasons why she shouldn't have listened, but she couldn't think of a single one. Instead she reached her arms up and slid them around his neck, seeing the shock in his blue eyes before they closed and his mouth settled softly on her lips.

"Yes," he whispered hungrily. His arms slid past her waist, bringing her against the length of his bare, warm body. "Yes, that's it, open your mouth...."

She did, letting his tongue probe inside and tangle with her own, feeling the hardness of his body, the sudden heat of him as he pinned her against the door.

"Eleanor," he breathed. His hips moved against her in undeniable need and urgency, and the kiss grew even more passionate—open mouths mingling fiercely together, voices breathing harshly, soft moans.

Eleanor whimpered as the old magic worked on her, as she felt her breasts crushing against his chest, her body aching to join with his. Her hands moved, searching out hard muscle and smooth flesh, working their way down his body, learning it with fingers that trembled softly.

"Yes," he groaned, drawing back, inviting her caresses. "Yes, touch me," he whispered shakily, opening his eyes to search hers. "Touch all of me, baby."

Insanity, she thought, but her hands were insistent, eager. She looked at him, watched the muscles ripple as her hands drew over them warmly, tenderly. He could have died—this might have been impossible. She thought that, and couldn't resist this once to know him, to possess him.

When her hands found and caressed his muscular stomach, he groaned and shuddered. She looked up at his hard, drawn face and exulted as she felt him tremble. He looked down at her, his eyes blazing with desire.

"I wish we were anywhere...except here," he said, his voice low and rough. "I want to do this to you. Touch you, with my eyes and my hands, in broad daylight. I want to be part of you."

"I'm afraid of you," Eleanor admitted at last, her eyes wide and vulnerable in her pale face.

"I'm sorry for that," he replied. "For so many things. I'd take back the past four years if I could. I'd start over with you."

"Once broken, a mirror is never the same."

"I could prove you wrong, if you'd let me," he said softly. "If you'd give me half a chance."

Eleanor closed her eyes in anguish. She wanted that, with him: wanted a new beginning. But there had been so much wounding, so much hurt.

"Come up to the house next Saturday and have lunch with us," he coaxed. "Mary June will be better by then; she'll do something pretty."

"Your houseguests will still be there," she reminded him.

"No, they damned well won't," he said shortly. "Not if I have to drive them to the airport. I've had pretty Maureen up to my neck! I'm sick of being chased. I like to do the chasing myself."

He always had. Now he was in pursuit of her, and once he caught her it would be just as it was before. Only this time she wouldn't recover.

He held her hands in his, searching her frightened, anxious eyes. "Trust me, just once. Just this once, Eleanor."

He sounded sincere. She knew she shouldn't believe him, but the sound of his voice was weakening her, as was this unnerving proximity to his unclothed body. He was so much a part of her already that nothing he did was unpleasant to her.

"All . . . right," she agreed reluctantly.

He smiled. "All right." His blue eyes twinkled. "Now kiss me and I'll get back in bed."

"Promise?" she asked breathlessly.

"Scout's honor." He tilted Eleanor's face up to his and brought his mouth down, then kissed her as she'd never been kissed before. It made her go hot all over with mingled, confusing emotions.

"Here," he whispered unsteadily. His hands caught hers, moving them to the back of his powerful thighs. "Now come close," he murmured against her mouth. "Come very, very close and let me feel you...."

His legs actually trembled when she obeyed him. Delicious, exquisite tingles of pleasure throbbed along her nerves as she felt his powerful body surge against her. She jerked a little and he smiled against her warm mouth.

"See how helpless I am with you?" he whispered. "Just like a boy, all hot and bothered and out of control. And I think it would embarrass me like hell with any other woman."

That was flattering. She sighed, then returned his kiss hungrily until he shuddered and gently eased her away.

He drew in a steadying breath, holding her by the waist as he searched her flushed face. Then he smiled slowly, wickedly. "Knocked the breath right out of you, didn't it? Same here."

"I . . . have to go," she faltered.

"You'd better fix your face first," he said, touching it with gentle fingers. "You look loved, little Ellie."

So did he. His red hair was disheveled, his mouth a little swollen, like her own. She felt the smile in her eyes, her lips, as she reached up and traced his eyebrows, his straight nose, his firm chin.

He brought her palms to his lips and kissed them. "That was the best medicine I've had since I was admitted," he whispered.

"And highly unethical it was, too," she teased. She moved discreetly away, her eyes fascinated by the beauty and symmetry of his body.

"It shouldn't embarrass you," he said quietly. "I don't feel like this with most women. I'm not ashamed of the way you affect me."

"No. I'm not, either," she said, surprising herself. She even managed to smile at him as he climbed back under the sheet and drew it up to his waist. "You're beautiful," she blurted out.

His warm eyes swept over her body. "So are you." Suddenly his face hardened. "Make love with me, Eleanor. Let me make the memories sweet. Let me show you how sweet it can be with a man who isn't a selfish brute."

"You weren't all that selfish," she murmured, embarrassed. "I was just inexperienced. I pushed you over the edge too soon."

"Another first," he replied. "Because you were the only woman I ever lost control with. Is that a shock, baby? It's the truth."

It was a shock. So was what she'd just let happen. She turned and went into his bathroom, smoothing her hair and wincing at the sight of her big dark eyes and swollen mouth. Well, she'd have to make a mad grab for her purse. Maybe Darcy wouldn't notice.

"You look fine," he said when she came out again. He held out his hand, and she went to him without a word, letting him press it to his mouth. "Come back and stay with me when you get off duty."

She started to agree, then remembered Wade. "I can't," she moaned. "Wade's taking me out to dinner."

His expression was indescribable. He hesitated a moment, then released her hand and leaned back against the pillows. "Granger again. Well, you can just break the date. I don't want you seeing him anymore."

"Oh, here we go again, slinging orders around like hash in a greasy spoon." She glared at him, stepping back. "Well, Mr. Taber, honey, you just lie here and give all the orders you like, but don't expect me to come to heel. I'm not your personal slave, despite your undeniable expertise at lovemaking. You won't seduce me a second time!"

"Won't I?" he challenged, bright-eyed. "Wait and see."

"You wait. I have work to do."

She whirled and stomped out the door, hating herself all over again for having trusted him in a moment of weakness.

Darcy pretended not to see the results of Keegan's mouth and hands, but she spent the rest of the day grinning.

"He wants to see you," she told Eleanor just before quitting time as she returned from answering Keegan's light.

"I'll have a photograph made, he can look at that. Look at the time!" Eleanor clucked. "I have to run. I'll give my report and see you tomorrow, darling. Have a nice evening."

"Eleanor, you can't strand me with him," Darcy wailed. "He doesn't like me!"

"That's all right. He doesn't like anybody," Eleanor assured her with a smile. "Just don't make any sudden moves, and you'll be fine. See you!"

Wade picked her up at six, and they went to a nice little Italian restaurant, but Eleanor's heart wasn't in it. She picked at her food and made halfhearted responses to Wade's teasing, and was thoroughly miserable.

"Is he getting to you, honey?" Wade asked sympathetically.

"He's just horrible," she muttered, "and I don't know why I can't manage to put him out of my mind and my life. I feel like such a wimp."

"It's called love," he told her. "A malady to which we are all vulnerable at one time or another. Chin up, girl, don't surrender now. We're just on the verge of victory!"

"Think so?" She sighed.

He grinned. "Well, I hear through the grapevine that the O'Clancys are on their way back to Ireland this very minute."

"Then as soon as Keegan is on his feet, he'll probably be right behind them," she replied.

"Care to bet? Unless I miss my guess, young lady, you're the target, not Maureen."

"Then he'd better be prepared for a long siege," she retorted.

"You said he invited you to lunch Saturday. Go. And while you're there, lay it on thick about how close you and I are getting," he added. "Then stand back and watch the fireworks."

The word "fireworks" brought back vivid memories of that afternoon—of practically swooning in Keegan's arms while he all but ravished her with his

mouth. She felt like someone in the grip of a savage
fever, burning up with unsatisfied longings, perish-
ing for lack of love. She had no strength at all anymore; Keegan, on the other hand, was very strong—
and single-minded.

"Save me from him," she pleaded.

"You don't need saving, beautiful girl," Wade
chuckled as he finished his coffee. "He does. You
wait. We've got him in a corner now."

"I wouldn't bet on that," she said. "He's slip-
pery. He doesn't really want to settle down."

"I think you're wrong. I think he wants that very
much. Why don't you listen to him for a change, Eleanor," he added quietly. "Ask some questions. Be
receptive. You might be astonished at the results you
get."

She shrugged, and the smile that touched her full
mouth was wistful. "All he'd want is an affair. I
don't need that."

"You need him," he told her. "How are you going
to survive without him? Honey, sometimes it takes a
compromise to satisfy both parties. You might think
about that."

"I don't mind compromise. But I'm not going the
whole way alone," she replied.

He lifted his coffee cup. "I don't think you'll have
to. I think very soon I may have to start looking
around for a new companion." He sighed. "And I'll
never find a girl like you again. I'd have Keegan
pushed out of an airplane if I thought it would get
me you. But I would like to see you happy. And I
don't think you'll ever find what you want with anyone except Keegan."

She was beginning to think that herself. It was kind of depressing, though. She watched Wade drive away an hour later, feeling as if her last friend had deserted her. He hadn't even fixed another date. He seemed to expect that she and Keegan would work it out, but she had reservations. Maureen might be out of the picture—but only temporarily, only until Keegan had satisfied his lust for Eleanor. There were too many differences socially and economically between the Tabers and the Whitmans for anything more permanent. And Eleanor didn't want a backstairs affair. Problem was, she admitted ruefully, she didn't know what to do anymore.

When she went on duty the next day, it was to find that Keegan had checked himself out the night before and gone home. It was a disappointment and a relief.

She worked her shift, dodged Darcy's questions and was emotionally exhausted by the time she went home. Her father was busy in his woodworking shop and didn't question her when she announced that she was going to take a nap before she cooked supper.

She was dreaming. She was being held and touched and loved, and she smiled as Keegan's face came into focus above hers. Then she realized with a start that it wasn't a dream. He was real.

"Don't panic," Keegan said with a soft, deep laugh as he lifted her from the bed in his arms. "I'm just going to take you up to the house to see my new colt."

"But . . . but I'm asleep," she protested drowsily, wiping her eyes with her hands.

"No, you aren't, pretty thing." His eyes wandered over her. She'd changed into white shorts and a pink button-up sleeveless blouse, and he loved the softness of her tanned body, the sweet weight in his arms. "God, you're pretty."

He bent and kissed her sleepy lips gently. "Wake up, beauty."

She linked her arms around his neck with a stifled yawn and buried her face in his throat. He smelled of Oriental cologne and soap, and she nuzzled closer.

"Don't do that," he said uneasily, "unless you want me to find a satisfying use for your bed."

Her breath caught. She was half-asleep and all too vulnerable, and suddenly the atmosphere in the room was hot and tense and full of promise.

"Your father went up to the house with my dad to see the colt," Keegan said, his voice deep and husky. "I told him I'd bring you along." He drew her closer. "It will take them half an hour to miss us.... Eleanor?"

She drew her head back to his shoulder and looked up at him, and she didn't have time to hide the hunger.

His eyes darkened, shifted to her breasts. She hadn't put on a bra, and he could see the dark, taut outline of her nipples. This wasn't how he'd planned it, but his body was in torment. He wanted her unbearably. And she wanted him.

"We could love each other on that bed," he whispered shakily, moving back toward it. "Cool sheets, hot bodies twisting together like twining vines. I can give you pleasure and watch you give yourself to me, Ellie. I can let you watch me go crazy when the time comes. Let me."

Keegan set her down on the sheet, holding her as he stripped away the coverlet, his eyes never leaving hers. Then he eased her back down, tossing the pillow to one side. His eyes burned with intent as his fingers slowly did away with buttons and pushed the blouse gently aside to bare her breasts.

He looked down and caught his breath at the mauve-and-pink perfection revealed there. She was fuller than she had been at eighteen, a vision. He reached down and touched the hard tips, rubbing them so that she trembled and bit her lip.

"Cry out, if you feel like it," he said huskily. "You can make all the noise you want to with me. No one will hear us."

Eleanor arched helplessly. He'd come along at the worst possible time, caught her at her most vulnerable. Years of repressed longing were freed at last, and the ensuing explosion of passion left her powerless to resist.

"Lift up," he said gently. "Let me undress you."

She let him do it; wide-eyed, she watched him, felt his warm, callused hands easily disposing of her shorts, her lacy briefs, until she lay revealed and yielding on the cool sheets.

Keegan brought her hands to his body, pressing them against him, holding her eyes with his. "Take my clothes off, Eleanor."

She didn't know where she found the courage. She'd never in her life undressed a man for this reason, not even Keegan. Most of all she remembered the pain, and her hands hesitated after she removed his shirt and let it drop to the floor.

He tilted her chin up until their eyes met. "It won't hurt this time," he promised. "This time is going to be everything your first time should have been."

She found the buckle of his belt, and even then she hesitated. He laughed softly at her fumbles and got to his feet.

"I'll do it this time," he murmured.

Keegan removed the rest of his clothing, while she watched him, fascinated. Then he turned and stretched out lazily beside her.

"And they say dreams don't come true," he whispered as his hands traveled sensuously up her rib cage to cup her breasts. "They do. Oh, yes, they do.... Turn over and lie against me, little one. I want to feel every inch of you touching my body."

He helped her, bending to kiss her open mouth as his hands moved up and down and around her soft, yielding body.

Eleanor lay still at first, accepting his caresses. But as Keegan found more intimate ways of touching her, she began to writhe. By the time his mouth had worked its way over her breasts and down her hips and thighs, she was crying.

Keegan had never aroused a woman to that state before. Most of them had been experienced, of course, and not as innocently accepting and eager as Eleanor. It excited him unbearably that she was so hungry for him. She must love him, he told himself. She wouldn't be so openly receptive to his loving if she didn't. The thought made him wild. He groaned against her stomach, and his fingers bit hard at her hips, lifting her.

"Want you," she whispered brokenly. Her eyes were closed, her head thrown back, her hands trembling on his hips. "I want you, want you!"

His mouth slid all the way up her body as he settled his weight along her legs and hips and breasts, feeling her soft body press deeply into the mattress. Eleanor trembled a little as he moved his body over hers, and he lifted his head to watch her, to make sure that he didn't hurt her.

"Shhh," he whispered reassuringly, brushing back her disheveled honey-brown hair. Her eyes were huge, frightened. "Relax for me, Ellie. Yes, like that, just relax and let me do the rest. Yes." He smiled softly, feeling the yielding, the warm softness enfolding him with delicious ease. He shifted closer, feeling her nails bite into his hips as she surged up against him with a gasp.

"Oh, God, this is going to be heaven," he whispered gruffly. "Don't be afraid, but it's going to get a little...rough...now, baby!" He groaned and shuddered as the fever began to burn in him. He clenched his hands under her hips, lifting her. "Baby, baby!"

Eleanor felt the rough movement of his body with a sense of awe, because it wasn't pain she was feeling. It was something unbearably sweet. Her eyes closed in an exquisite shudder as he touched her in a way that made her body ripple with pleasure.

"Yes...do that," she pleaded against his suddenly devouring mouth. "Yes, like that, like that! Keegan!"

She was crying now, whimpering, her soft hands clutching at his hips, his thighs, working magic on the long, damp sleekness of his back as his body rose and fell with hers in the sunlit silence of the bedroom.

Keegan never remembered what happened next. Eleanor was crying and he was on a roller coaster that he couldn't stop. He cried out above her, his voice like that of someone in torment. His body arched like a bow, and his face contorted in exquisite agony as he cried her name.

She reached up, drawing him down against her, comforting him, because she was blazing with tenderness and fulfilled desire, her face wet with tears.

"Keegan," she whispered in wonder. Her lips touched his face, his eyes, his cheeks, his trembling mouth. She smiled. "Keegan."

"Thank you," he whispered shakily. "Thank you for trusting me, for giving yourself so sweetly. I never knew peace, until now. I had to show you, teach you, that it can be magic. A man and a woman can touch the sky."

"Lovemaking," she whispered. Her eyes closed. "You're my lover."

"I've always been your lover," he murmured. "Only me. You've never known anyone else like this, have you?"

"No." She stretched and sighed as he rolled away and leaned over her, smiling.

"Now let's go see my colt," he murmured. "And I'll feed you supper."

She'd wanted something more loverlike than that, and she had to force herself not to ask for it. Could he have loved her that way without feeling something for her? She didn't think so.

"All right," she said. "I'll get dressed."

"What a crime, to cover a body like that," he murmured, watching her put her clothes back on. "My God, just touching you drove me crazy."

"You look pretty good yourself," she said demurely.

Keegan got up with a sigh and put his own clothing back on. When he finished, he pulled Eleanor close and held her against him for a long moment.

"I didn't think," he said quietly. "You aren't on the pill, I gather?"

She swallowed. "No."

He lifted his head, searching her eyes. "If we made a baby, I'll take care of you," he said, his voice deep and quiet.

Eleanor actually blushed. She pushed away from him because it sounded as if he had something other than marriage in mind. "We'd better get up to the farm," she said evasively.

He studied her straight back, frowning.

"I didn't get pregnant before," she pointed out without looking at him. "There's probably nothing to worry about."

"There could be, if it happens again."

"It won't," she said firmly, and walked into the hall. "One lapse doesn't make an affair, Keegan."

"I don't want an affair," he growled.

"Yes, I know." She went out the front door, Keegan at her heels.

"Wait a minute," he said shortly. "Let's get this ironed out right now, Eleanor. You've got it all wrong!"

"No, I haven't!" she returned fiercely. "You have. I'm a grown woman now, not a child. You won't own me by seducing me!"

He seemed at a loss for words. He started to speak, stopped, tried again. "I didn't plan what happened," he said softly. "I didn't mean it to happen...."

"You never do." She laughed coldly. "I'm just handy. Handy, and stupid!"

He grimaced. She didn't understand! She thought he was using her. "For God's sake, it's not like that!" he burst out. "Please, baby, listen to me!"

"Look, there's Dad," she said, watching Gene Taber drive toward the house with her father in the car. She flushed, thinking what they'd have interrupted minutes before. Now, however, she was grateful for the interruption. She couldn't even look at Keegan. How would she ever be able to sleep in that bedroom again?

Ten

I forgot my pipe." Barnett Whitman grinned. "Can't get my ideas together without it, not if I'm going to build a halfway decent barn. Pretty colt, Eleanor, you ought to go up and see it."

"That's where we're headed," said Keegan. He caught Eleanor's unresponsive hand in his.

"Wait, I have to change," she protested.

"I have seen a woman's legs before," Gene Taber teased.

"But it's so informal," she persisted.

"Don't you have a wraparound skirt?" Keegan asked.

Now how had he known that? She nodded and rushed off to drag it out of her closet. She wouldn't let herself think. She didn't dare. There would be time enough for regrets later.

She drew on her white wraparound skirt and tied it, filing out the door just behind her father. Keegan came up to her as she stopped on the porch, and he held out his hand, watching, waiting. With a faint sigh, she put her own into it and felt his fingers contract, warm and possessive.

He smiled.

"Come on," he said, leading her to the car. "We'll drive up behind them."

"You look better," she murmured.

"Since I left the hospital, I expect you mean?" he asked dryly, smiling as she blushed. "Yes, I feel better, too. I never did thank you, did I, for telling Dad what to do."

"He was upset," she said.

He helped her into the passenger seat of the red Porsche. "So were you, I hear," he said, noting her downcast expression as he closed the door.

Eleanor leaned back as she fastened her seatbelt and waited for him to get in and start the engine. Gene Taber had already driven off in his green Buick with Barnett beside him. It seemed the day for a family get-together, but all she wanted to do was...was stay with Keegan and never leave him, she admitted miserably. She couldn't bear the thought of being alone again, of being without him for the rest of her life. Especially now. And what if she did get pregnant?

Involuntarily, her fingers went to her waist, pressing there in wonder as they drove up toward Flintlock. A baby would be nice. Someone to love and care for, someone to look after and fuss over. She smiled.

The man beside her saw that smile and where her fingers were resting, and he smiled, too. He began to whistle softly, glancing sideways at her and smiling.

She glanced at him and looked away again. Smug, wasn't he? she thought bitterly. He'd had his way, and now he was satisfied. He'd be off in search of a new conquest.

"The colt is out of Main Chance, by Straightaway," he told her. "A Triple Crown winner if I've ever seen one. Beautiful conformation."

"Wasn't Straightaway the reason you escaped from the hospital?" she asked slyly.

"I had to. O'Clancy damned near took him home." Keegan pulled into his driveway and followed his father's car back to the garage, pulling in beside the Buick. "Feeling all right?" he asked unexpectedly, his blue eyes concerned as they searched her face.

"Of . . . of course," she faltered.

"I didn't hurt you, did I?" he asked, his voice softer than satin.

She shook her head, and he nodded, apparently satisfied. He got out and helped her out.

"We're going to look over the layout for the barn," Gene told them. "Barnett swears he's up to it. Then we'll meet you in the house for supper. Mary June's fixing ham, by the way. She swore up and down that we'd never see another piece of chicken as long as we live after your near miss, son."

Keegan chuckled as he locked Eleanor's fingers in his. "Suits me. I think I'll sell my stock in that chicken packing plant we own shares of, too."

"I don't blame you, boy." Barnett grinned.

The older men wandered off across the yard, and Keegan drew Eleanor along with him into the spacious stable with its wide, woodchip-covered aisle. He stopped at a middle stall and pushed Eleanor in front of him so that she could look over the gate. There, in the stall, was a sleek, beautiful brown mare with a small, spindly-legged colt.

"Isn't he a beauty?" he asked proudly. He put his hands on her shoulders, idly stroking them. "A fine young devil, all nerves right now. He'll be a sight to behold in a few months."

"He's a champion all right." She sighed. "I've always loved horses, even if I don't know one bloodline from another."

"I could teach you that," he said, his breath fanning her hair. "I could teach you anything you wanted to know. And before you fly at me," he added when she turned, glaring, "I don't mean sex."

That stopped her. She stared up at him breathlessly, her whole body reacting in sensuous pleasure to the intensity of his gaze.

"For God's sake, don't look at me like that," he said harshly. "Don't you realize even now the way you affect me?"

She didn't, but when he drew her against his long, lean body, she got the message.

"Don't pull away," he said quietly. "You belong to me now. You know everything there is to know about my body and how it responds." He smiled at her warmly. "Besides, you're a nurse."

"That doesn't make me any more confident, actually," she confessed. Her hands touched his chest through the shirt and she felt him shudder as his heartbeat increased. She pressed her fingers against him, feeling the soft, bristly pressure of chest hair through the material, feeling him stiffen. She looked up, fascinated by the newness of the relationship they were sharing, by what had happened.

"How do things stand between you and Granger?" he asked.

She shifted restlessly. "I don't have to tell you that."

He tipped her chin up and searched her eyes. "After this afternoon, I have the right to know," he replied. "You gave me something Granger's never had from you."

Something he would never have, but she couldn't tell him that. She bit her lower lip. "I'm very fond of Wade," she said, which was true. She studied his shirt button.

"And how do you feel about me?" he asked.

"I . . . want you," she confessed, closing her eyes. Well, it was the truth, after all. She did want him. But she wasn't about to tell him the rest of it, that she loved him and she'd never get over him. She'd experienced him totally as a man, and her heart was now his.

His hands smoothed up and down her bare arms, strong, warm, possessive hands. "Only want, Eleanor?" he probed.

She lifted her dark eyes to his. "What are you waiting for, another breathless confession of undying love?" she asked with a harsh laugh. "Wouldn't that be history repeating itself? Isn't physical desire enough for you, Keegan? We're both adults, after all. And I'm sure you're relieved to know that I'm not going to throw my heart at your feet a second time."

He flinched slightly, then lowered his eyes and looked down at her hands, still pressed tautly against his chest.

"Wouldn't you like to try loving me again?" he asked softly. He lifted his eyes back to hers, searching them in silence. "I might be a better proposition this go-around," he remarked at last. "God knows, we're both more mature now."

Eleanor squared her chin and stared at him for a moment. Then, "Desire isn't enough to build a relationship on," she said. "You told me that four years ago, don't you remember?" She laughed bitterly.

His eyes closed. "I remember."

"You did try to be kind, I realize that," she acknowledged. "But you were in love with Lorraine, and you couldn't disguise it. If I'd been a little less infatuated . . ."

Keegan let her go and turned away to light a cigarette, his back to her. Then he looked up toward the ceiling. "Are you trying to get back at me, Ellie? Is that what this evasion is all about?"

"No, it isn't," she replied. "I'm trying to tell you that what I want now is a stable relationship with a man, some security and a future that doesn't involve stolen moments in the back seat of a car or a deserted house."

"Oh, God," he cried, bowing his head. "Oh, God, why won't you listen to me?" He turned, his blue eyes dark with pain, and something like defeat. "I'm not offering you some clandestine affair!"

"I don't care," she forced herself to say calmly. "Wade's asked me to marry him." She watched that register, and nodded. "And after today, I'll say yes,

Keegan. Because I can't risk letting what happened today repeat itself. I can't seem to say no to you. So I'll settle for a permanent relationship instead.''

"You won't be able to give him what you gave me," he said, his voice harsh.

"Of course I won't. But I'll take care of him, and be there when he needs me. I'll have everything I want, and I'll give him children.''

He looked as if she'd cut him with a knife. Abruptly he turned away, his eyes blank and unseeing, his soul in agony. So he'd been wrong. She didn't love him. She only wanted him, after all, and she was so afraid of giving in again that she'd even rush into marriage with a man she didn't love to keep him out of her life. What a horrible, bitter irony: he'd pushed her away when she'd offered him her love, and now that he wanted it, he couldn't get it back. Irony.

"Then I guess that's all there is," he said, his voice dull, lifeless.

"That's all there is," she agreed. She turned away from the stall and walked outside into the sunlight.

Keegan followed her with eyes as cold as death. She was like quicksilver, he thought blankly, impossible to catch and hold. If only he hadn't rushed her, if only he'd held back this afternoon. But he'd wanted her so desperately. He'd thought it would solve everything, show her how he felt about her. All it had done was to push her into a loveless marriage.

"I'd rather not stay for supper," she said when he joined her at the front porch.

"If you leave now, they'll wonder why you left."

She grimaced. "Yes, I suppose so."

He searched her pale face quietly, the smoking cigarette in his hand all but forgotten. "I'm sorry," he said. "Sorry for it all. For the past, for the present. Even for the future. All I seem to do is hurt you, when that's the last thing I've ever wanted to do."

"You haven't hurt me," she said, folding her arms across her breasts. "I was hardly a victim, either time."

"I seduced you," he said, staring down at the cigarette.

"No!" She touched his arm hesitantly, searching his tormented face. "Oh, no, it wasn't seduction. Not ever. I wanted you."

"What will we do if you get pregnant?" he asked softly. "Will you tell Granger the truth?"

"If I get pregnant, I..." She couldn't go on with the lie. "I don't know what I'll do, except that I'll have it," she finished lamely.

He started to touch her face, his fingers slightly unsteady. "I can't lose you twice," he whispered.

She frowned. "I don't understand."

"I..." he began.

"It's on the table!" Mary June called out the front door. "Hurry up before I throw it out!"

"Damn," Keegan muttered with a sigh. He ground out his cigarette under his heel. "Oh, well, maybe it's for the best," he said gruffly. "Come on." He guided her up the steps, leaving her to ponder what he'd said.

"Thank God we can sit down to table in peace, with the O'Clancys gone," Gene Taber declared jovially as Mary June began serving dinner. "There were nights when I was almost certain that Maureen was going to drag Keegan under the table and rape him between courses."

Keegan glanced at his father with a faint smile. "I felt that way myself a time or two," he murmured. "She was a bit forward for my taste."

"I had the same fears for Eleanor when Wade came to dinner," Barnett Whitman announced, glancing at her with a broad grin. "He was practically drooling the first time."

Keegan banged his cup on the table, looking grim, as Eleanor flushed and Gene and Barnett exchanged discreet smiles.

"Here it is," Mary June interrupted, her black eyes flashing as she put a platter of ham on the table. "No more chicken around this here house," she added with a glare at Keegan. "I never seen the like. Folks trying to kill themselves with chicken poison...."

Keegan glared back at her. "I was not trying to commit suicide."

"Any fool who'd put cooked chicken back on the same plate with uncooked chicken pieces deserves just what he gets!" Mary June retorted.

"Miss Perfection," Keegan returned, "haven't you ever made a mistake?"

"Yes, sir," she agreed. "Saying yes when Mr. Gene asked if I wanted to work for him!"

"Stop it, you two," Gene roared, banging the table with his fist. "Can't we have just one peaceful meal in this house without the two of you coming to blows?"

Mary June sniffed. "I don't start it. He does."

"Ha!" Keegan shot back.

"I'll just go and put that chocolate cake I just baked in the trash can," the cook threatened, lips pursed mutinously.

Keegan sighed. He picked his white napkin up out of his lap and waved it back and forth.

Mary June nodded curtly. "Good enough for you," she said. "And see you stay out of my kitchen from now on, if you please. I don't want folks trying to kill themselves in there. Spoils my pantry, it does."

Keegan glared at her retreating back as she hobbled away. "Someday," he threatened. "Someday!"

"Shhhh!" Gene hissed at him. "She'll quit!"

Keegan grinned. "Is there hope?"

"Well, we'd die if we had to depend on your culinary skills, and that's a fact," he told his son.

"Just because I put the damned chicken in the wrong place . . ." he muttered.

"You should have married Maureen, while you had the chance," Eleanor said with a forced smile. "She'd have baked you cakes."

"She couldn't even buy a decent cake, much less make one from scratch," Keegan said venomously, his eyes narrowed. "And I can pick my own wife, thank you."

Of course he could—some society woman with a family tree as monied as his own. Eleanor smiled faintly at her plate as she tried to eat.

"I wish you'd marry somebody," Gene told his son. "I'm getting old enough to crave grandchildren."

"Adopt," Keegan advised him. He glanced quickly at Eleanor, then looked away again. "I like my freedom."

Eleanor didn't look up, but her heart felt as if it had been cut in two. It was the truth, of course: he didn't want to marry anybody. But why throw it in her face now, of all times, after she'd given in to him?

"He's baiting you, girl," Gene said.

She looked up to find Keegan grinning at her.

"I don't care if he dies an old maid," she said bluntly.

"Heartless woman," Keegan muttered. He finished his meal and sat back in his chair with a long sigh. Why not bring it out into the open? he mused. He could gain an ally or two, and he needed them.

"Why don't you marry me and make an honest man out of me?" he asked her bluntly.

Her fork clattered wildly as it hit the china plate. She retrieved it clumsily, red-faced and breathless as all eyes suddenly focused on her.

"Beast!" she exclaimed.

He pursed his lips and studied her with that possessive smile she hated. "Why not marry me? I'm sexy and filthy rich, I can kiss you stupid without half trying, and you'd get half of the colt to boot."

Gene and Barnett stared at her as she searched for some graceful way out.

"You can't cook," she declared.

"You could teach me," he returned.

"I'm going to marry Wade," she announced defiantly.

"Over my dead body," he replied fiercely. "You're not getting yourself tied to that playboy!"

"Look who's calling Wade a playboy!" she cried. "And you're one to talk about him doing it hanging from tree limbs, when you tried it in a hospital room with nurses coming and going all around us!"

"Eleanor," he chided, nodding toward their fascinated audience, which now included Mary June, "how could you embarrass me like this?"

"I couldn't embarrass you by taking off your clothes in Central Park!"

He smiled slowly. "I'm game if you are. I'll rush right out and buy two plane tickets to New York."

She threw up her hands and got out of the chair. "I give up."

"Marry me, Eleanor, or I'll hound you day and night," he threatened.

She flushed and turned away. "I'm going home."

"I'll drive you."

"No, you won't!" she raged, close to tears. How could he humiliate her like this? She loved him, and he was making some horrible joke out of it.

He saw the tears and wondered if there could be some deep, lingering passion there, if she still cared for him. She was upset, but she wasn't unreceptive. He had her on the run. If he played his hand carefully, he might yet wrench her out of Wade's arms and get her to a minister.

"If you're determined, we'll all go," Gene said, grinning. "Come on, Barnett."

"I won't ride with him," Eleanor said, pointing at Keegan.

Keegan sighed theatrically. "Shoved aside by the woman of my dreams. I'll perish to death for love of you, Eleanor."

"The only thing you'll perish of is your own cooking," she said curtly. "I'm going home. Good night."

She didn't say another word to him. She crawled in the back of Gene's car, and the two older men talked farm business all the way back.

Once home, Eleanor went straight to bed. And that was the worst thing she could have done. The bed still smelled of Keegan, and it always would. She'd been able to strip off and change the bed linen, but she'd never be able to erase the memories... and they haunted her dreams.

Eleven

If Eleanor thought she'd seen the last of Keegan for a while, she was in for a surprise. When she went down to fix breakfast the next morning, he was sitting in the living room with her father, as relaxed as if he belonged there.

He looked up as she entered the room and grinned at her. "Good morning, glory," he teased. "You look pretty in that."

"That" referred to her faded blue jeans and a green pullover knit shirt. Eleanor was off duty today and hadn't expected to find Keegan piled up in the living room like a redheaded snake, just waiting for her.

Now she felt her face going red as she looked at him, remembering yesterday and how easily she'd succumbed. Keegan saw her flush and smiled even wider.

"I wasn't expecting you," she said helplessly.

"I figured that," he replied. "What are we having for breakfast?"

"Did Mary June's ankle get worse?" she asked sarcastically.

"Nope. I just like your biscuits," he chuckled. "And your sweet company, pretty girl."

"She is pretty," Barnett agreed solemnly. "I never could understand why she stayed single so long."

"She was waiting for me, of course," Keegan declared, leaning back in his chair like a conquering general. "Weren't you, Ellie?"

"Don't call me Ellie," she grumbled.

"Okay, honey."

She started to protest, then threw up her hands and went to make breakfast.

Keegan watched her through bacon and eggs and buttered biscuits and homemade apple butter, and she fidgeted helplessly in her chair. After all that had happened between them, she couldn't be casual about their relationship. She just didn't understand what he wanted of her.

"Want to go watch a harness race with me?" he asked Eleanor as she sipped coffee. "Or we could go to the yearling sale at Gainesmore Farm; I saw an Arabian over there that I'd like to bid on."

She cocked her head, puzzled. "You know I'm not that smart about horses, although I'm sure you think that's unspeakable for someone born in Lexington."

"Okay," he relented, "how about a walk in the woods? Or you could get your father's fishing pole and we'll go drown some worms."

"I . . . I have to work in the garden today," she faltered. "The weeds are killing my tomatoes."

He pursed his lips and shrugged. "So we'll hoe out the tomatoes," he said quietly. "I'm not all that particular about what we do, as long as we do it together."

Barnett Whitman was grinning from ear to ear. He finished his coffee and got up. "I have to go over some blueprints with Gene," he said, beaming at them. "I'm back on the job as of today. My doctor said it was all right, before you start screaming, Eleanor," he added.

She lifted an eyebrow. "Did I say anything?"

"No, and see that you don't," he chuckled. "See you later, kids."

"I'll bet it's been years since anyone called you a kid," Eleanor said after her father had driven away.

"Years since I've felt like one, surely," he agreed. He folded his forearms on the table and searched her face. "Do you really want to spend the day hoeing weeds?"

She glared at him. "No, I won't go to bed with you, if that was the next and very obvious question."

"It wasn't, actually, although I'd rather sleep with you than eat," he said softly, his blue eyes smiling into hers. "You and I do something incredible together when we make love."

Eleanor stared at the coffee cup she was holding. Her heart was going wild, all because he was using that slow, sexy tone she remembered so well.

"I keep wondering what would have happened if I hadn't given in to temptation that night four years ago," he said absently.

"You'd probably have married Lorraine and lived happily ever after," she said dully.

"Do you think so? I don't." He got up, dragged a cigarette from the pocket of his blue-plaid shirt and lit it. "The only thing Lorraine and I had in common was that we both thought she was a knockout."

"All the same, she fit into your life-style very well."

He turned, leaning back against the sink. "So do you," he said quietly.

She laughed. "Not me," she returned, toying with the cup. "I don't know about horses, and I'm certainly not debutante material."

"You're real, though," he said, forcing her to meet his gaze. "That's right. You're honest and stubborn, and you don't back away from things. You have qualities I admire, Ellie. The economics don't matter a damn. They never have."

"They matter to me," she replied shortly. "Look around you, Keegan. This is a nice house, thanks to you and your father, but it's not a patch on Flintlock. I've never worn fancy clothes until recently, and I didn't even know that a champagne buffet meant hors d'oeuvres and drinks. When I first walked onto Wade's property, his mother and sister came at me like spears...."

"Just as I thought," he said darkly. "I've known them for years."

"I gave as good as I got, thank you," she told him, "but the fact is, I don't fit in that kind of society. You were right in the first place when you were warning me off Wade. I'm just a country girl who might someday make a small mark in the nursing profession. But as a—" she searched for a discreet term "—companion for a rich man, I'd be a dead loss."

"I'm not in the market for a mistress," he said, his voice like velvet.

Her eyebrows arched. "Excuse me, but isn't that the position you're offering me? Or do you make a habit of seducing anyone who happens to be handy?"

He sighed wearily as he lifted the cigarette to his mouth. "Eleanor," he said, "what am I going to do about you?"

"You might just leave me alone," she replied, although the thought hurt dreadfully. Still, it was the most sensible course.

"I can't." He held out his hand. "Come walking, Ellie. I want to talk."

She hesitated, but he nodded curtly and she yielded. This would be the last time she obeyed, she promised herself. The very last time.

She took his outstretched hand and followed him out into the sunshine. He locked her fingers with his and went off down a path beside the fence that led to the stream cutting through his property.

"Four years ago," he said without looking at her, "I came by your house on your birthday and asked you out. That night, when I picked you up, you were wearing a blue print dress with puffy sleeves and a low neckline. Your hair was down around your shoulders and smelled of gardenias. I gave you supper at an exclusive restaurant and then I drove you out to the river and parked on a deserted stretch of dirt road."

"Keegan..."

"Shhh," he said gently. He turned her as they reached the shade of a towering oak tree and held her by the arms, studying her face. "And then I started kissing you. And you kissed me back. I put my hand under your bodice and you held it there. We started kissing feverishly then, and somehow I got you into the back seat of that big Lincoln and eased you down, and you let me take your clothes off. It was a warm, clear night, and we made love to the sound of crickets and rushing water, and afterward you told me that you loved me."

She lowered her eyes to his chest. "It isn't kind, reminding me," she whispered miserably.

"I'm not doing it to torment you, Eleanor," he said. "I want to make you understand how I felt. You were barely eighteen, not even a full-grown woman, and a virgin to boot. I was considerably older, practically engaged to Lorraine, and I was torn apart with conflicting emotions. I never meant it to happen at all, but once you let me touch you, I couldn't stop."

"I realize I was as much to blame as you were, Keegan," she replied. "I was crazy about you. I thought, since you were asking me out, that you'd stopped caring about Lorraine and I had a chance with you." She laughed hollowly. "I should have realized that a man like you wouldn't want a shy little country mouse when he could have a fairy princess like Lorraine, but then, I wasn't thinking."

He ground his cigarette out under his heel and took her face in his lean, warm hands. "I never slept with Lorraine," he said, his voice deep and soft. "Part of what I felt for her was sexual. Probably most of it was. Once I had you, though, I wasn't able to want her. That was why I drove her away. I had nothing left to give."

She looked deeply into his blue eyes and was shaken by what she saw. "When you told me why you'd asked me out, I wanted to die," she confessed finally. "I'd practically thrown myself at you.... It was humiliating."

"Not to me," he murmured. "All my life, women had chased me because I was rich. You were the first, and the last, to want me just for myself."

She smiled softly. "You were very special."

"So were you." He bent and kissed her, tenderly, warmly. His mouth opened and poised there; she could taste the smoke on his breath. "Your body haunted me after you left Lexington. Your face. Your voice. I couldn't sleep for feeling your body under mine, those sweet little cries that pulsed out of you. Do you know even now how it excites me to hear you moan when I make love to you?"

"You make it so... so wild," she faltered.

"So do you, honey," he replied curtly. His hands tangled in her thick, soft hair, and he tugged at it. "You make it so much more than a merging of bodies. I think about babies when I take you, Eleanor, did you know?" he whispered, and his mouth found hers even as the words registered in her whirling mind.

She gripped his forearms, trembling as he deepened the kiss; then his eyes opened and stared straight into hers.

"Come close," he said against her mouth.

"I'll hurt you," she whispered hesitantly.

"Yes." He reached down and moved her legs until they touched his, then his eyes closed and his mouth crushed hers in a silence blazing with promise.

He bent, holding the kiss, and lifted her into his arms. "Just once more," he whispered, his voice deep and husky as he carried her into the shade of the tree and placed her gently on the ground. "Just one more time, Eleanor...."

He stretched out against her, and the kiss grew urgent, passionate. His hands caressed her pliant body, molding her breasts, her rib cage, her waist and stomach, her long legs.

"No," she moaned. Her hands pushed halfheartedly at his chest, until they found an opening and pressed into warm, hard muscle and thick hair. His tongue searched inside her mouth, and she felt his heart shaking her with its feverish beat, felt the crush of his body over hers, twisting her against the hard ground as he gave up his control to the passion driving him.

"You want me," he whispered huskily. "I want you. What else matters?"

"I won't...be used," she whimpered. "I won't!"

"Here," he said under his breath, moving her hand against his chest. "Touch me like this."

"Oh, Keegan, this won't...solve anything." She panted, twisting her face away from his.

"Yes, it will," he said. He slid down against her, feverishly pushing up the hem of her shirt, revealing her bare, taut breasts. "God, Ellie, you've got the prettiest breasts," he whispered huskily, then bent his head.

She was lost from the first touch of his open mouth, taking her inside that warm, moist darkness, letting her feel the roughness of his tongue, the soft nip of his teeth. He whispered something she didn't hear, and his lean hands smoothed warmly up and down her rib cage while his mouth made her tremble.

He worked his way down to the fastening of her jeans, pressing his face into her warm flesh, making her burn and ache. His fingers dug into her hips, lifting her rhythmically to the probing of his tongue, the nip of his teeth.

"Please," she whispered helplessly. Her eyes closed and she shuddered. Her hands held his hair, trapping his mouth against her warm belly. "Please, make me stop aching."

"There's only one way to do that," he whispered. He slid up her body, his mouth poised over hers as his hands found and cupped her breasts. He searched her eyes in a lingering scrutiny. "Tell me you love me, Eleanor, and I'll love you in ways you'll never forget as long as you live. I'll make you cry."

"Please." She was beyond arguing. Her body throbbed, burned. She arched helplessly, her legs moving in a wild rhythm on the ground. "Keegan . . ."

"Say the words, baby," he breathed, toying with the zipper of her jeans. "Come on. Tell me, Ellie."

Her eyes closed. Why not? He owned her, after all. He owned her. "I love you," she whispered achingly, her eyes opening, large and dark and full of pain. "I always have. I always will."

He hesitated, his lips parting, his body shuddering as he looked down at her.

"Isn't that the price?" she whispered brokenly. She lifted her body, sliding her arms under his to press her breasts hungrily against his chest. "Oh,

Lord, how sweet it feels to do that," she moaned softly. She rubbed her torso against his and felt him tremble at the silken brush of her skin. "I want you. I want all of you, right here, under the sun, I want to look up and watch you having me...."

His mind exploded. He stripped her with hands that trembled, then shrugged off his own clothing and overwhelmed her with feverish abandon.

She laughed. Laughed, as he held her down and forced his body on hers, and she matched that wild passion, every step of the way. Her eyes open, huge, blazing with the same hunger he was feeling, watched him, gloried in what he did to her with his hands, his mouth, his powerful body.

"I love you," she cried in a voice she barely recognized. Then, as the tension accelerated into something like flying, she felt her body tensing until it threatened to shatter. Her fingers dug into his back while he arched over her and ground her into the dead leaves and grass with the feverish crush of his muscular body.

"Yes, watch me," she said shakily. "Watch me!"

The leaves above them blurred and burst into color. She felt her mouth open, her body turn to liquid and burn with lightning flashes as she throbbed and throbbed and throbbed. She could hardly see his face above her.

"Eleanor," he moaned.

Her fingers trembled as they found his and locked with them. "You belong to me," she whispered.

"Oh, God, yes." His eyes closed and his head fell beside her ear, tortured breaths pulsating out of him with strangled groans as his body tensed and convulsed. "I...love...you!"

It was the passion talking, of course; she knew that, but it was so sweet to hold him, to soothe him, and know that what she'd given him he could find with no one else. For this tiny stretch of time, he was completely, wholly hers.

He trembled in her arms for a long time. And this time, there was no lazy awakening, no moving quickly away. He collapsed against her and lay breathing raggedly until she could feel his skin sticking to hers.

"Yes, hold me, Eleanor," he whispered. One lean hand came up to trace her ear, her cheek, to smooth her damp hair. Somewhere in the tree above them, birds sang sweetly. "Hold me, now."

"Are you all right?" she asked softly.

"Yes. Are you?"

She smiled against his tanned cheek. "I don't know."

He managed to raise himself enough to search her eyes. His were very blue, sated, full of secrets and adoration. Genuine adoration.

"I never stopped loving you," he whispered, kissing her shocked eyes closed. "I didn't realize that I did until it was too late, until I'd driven you away with my own confused indifference. And then I couldn't get you back. I couldn't get to you."

"You love me?" she asked uncertainly.

He lifted his head and touched her mouth softly with his. "You can ask that, after the way I just made love to you?" he whispered.

"Desire..." She faltered.

"Physical love," he corrected quietly. "Because that's what it is, between you and me. It always was, even the first time. I'll never get enough of you."

"But you let me go," she said uncertainly.

He kissed her forehead with lips that were breathlessly tender. "I had to," he said simply. "I'd managed to foul up my whole life by getting myself engaged to Lorraine. I had to force her to break the engagement, and by then you were settled in Louisville. I did write to you, but you wouldn't answer me. I couldn't blame you for that, after the way I'd treated you. But it was a damned long four years, Eleanor."

"You never were trying to make a convenience of me, were you?" she asked wonderingly. "It was this, from the beginning, from the day I came home again."

He nodded, his eyes quiet and sad. "I loved you so much, little one. And every attempt I made to come close just pushed you farther away."

"I didn't know," she said.

"Yes, I realized that. And then Wade Granger started coming around," he said curtly. "And I wanted to kill him."

"He saw through me very quickly," she confessed. "He was my best friend. He knew how I felt about you. He took me out to try and make you jealous."

"He succeeded," he said, his voice quiet. "I was terrified of losing you to him. Especially after yesterday. I lost my head once I got you in my arms in that bedroom. I couldn't have stopped to save my life. And then you said you were going to marry him...."

"He'd have been shocked," she said with a slow smile. "I'd already refused him. It was all a last-ditch attempt to save myself from you."

"And look where it got you," he mused, lifting his head to look down at their locked bodies.

She flushed. "Keegan!"

"You're not embarrassed?" he teased. "Not after the way you were with me this time?"

She swallowed. "Actually, yes, I am. And for heaven's sake, what if someone should come along?"

He sighed ruefully. "We could go inside, and do this in a bed," he said. "Or," he added with a wicked grin as he lifted himself away from her, "we could drive into town and get a marriage license."

Eleanor sat up, gaping at him as he dragged on his jeans and tossed hers over to her.

"Don't look so shocked," he murmured. "Don't you want to marry me? You'd get to sleep in my arms every night. You could even have a son or two with me, if you liked."

She was still gaping. With a resigned sigh, he stuffed her deftly back into her clothing and laughed at her shocked expression.

"A fine lot of help you are," he muttered as he pulled the knit shirt back over her taut breasts. "Shameless woman."

"I'm...speechless," she faltered. "You really want to marry me?"

"Didn't you hear what I told you while we were making love?" he asked. "I love you. What I have in mind is a lifelong affair, not a hurried roll in the hay. I want children with you, you little idiot!"

"Oh."

"Legitimate children," he emphasized. "And don't think I didn't see the way you touched your waist and grinned yesterday. You could already be pregnant. I have a feeling I'm not sterile."

She glanced at him shyly. "I may not fit into your world."

"I'll make a new one, just for us," he replied. He lifted her to her feet and framed her face with his hands. "I love you," he said fervently. "Deathlessly, with all my heart. I want to live with you until I die, and I hope we have sixty years and that when the time comes, we go down into the dark locked in each other's arms. Because I'm afraid of nothing in this world except trying to live in it without you."

Tears stung her eyes as he bent and drew her lips warmly under his. "I feel the same way," she whispered shakily. "I never stopped loving you. There could never have been anyone else. I gave you my heart, and I couldn't get it back."

"Then let's get married," he said.

She smiled. "If you're sure."

"Of course I'm sure," he murmured, smiling. "I'm getting tired of finding excuses to come down here every day. Marry me and we can stay at Flintlock and Mary June will get your breakfast."

"Who'll get Dad's?" she asked suddenly.

"We'll get him a maid of his very own," he chuckled. "Someone who'll make a good nanny as well, when we come visiting."

"Oh, darling," she whispered, lifting her arms around his neck.

"Oh, yes," he murmured, and his strong hands tugged her up against his body in a fierce embrace. "Kiss me once more, and we'll go up to the house and break the news to all concerned. I'll even call your friend Wade and tell him."

"How generous of you," she teased.

"I can afford to be generous now." He kissed her softly. "I've got the whole world in my arms."

She sighed. "I've just thought of something," she said, hesitating.

"What?"

"Darling, all our children will have freckles," she murmured.

He laughed. "Shut up and kiss me."

She was still smiling when he parted her lips with his. As she returned the kiss, Eleanor reflected that she didn't really mind the prospect of freckled children with red hair. They'd stand out in a crowd, just like their handsome redheaded father.

She remembered reading somewhere that revenge was like the eye of a tiger, seeing with narrow vision. She'd seen Keegan that way, hating him for what he'd done to her. But now it all seemed worthwhile. Her tiger had blue eyes, and although she'd never get him into a cage, she was perfectly content to run free with him. She closed her eyes, sighing softly as she touched his cheek with her left hand. In her mind, she could already see the thin gold band he would slide on her third finger, a circle of love without end.

AMERICAN TRIBUTE

Where a man's dreams count for more than his parentage...

Look for these upcoming titles under the Special Edition American Tribute banner.

CHEROKEE FIRE
Gena Dalton #307—May 1986
It was Sabrina Dante's silver spoon that Cherokee cowboy Jarod Redfeather couldn't trust. The two lovers came from opposite worlds, but Jarod's Indian heritage taught them to overcome their differences.

NOBODY'S FOOL
Renee Roszel #313—June 1986
Everyone bet that Martin Dante and Cara Torrence would get together. But Martin wasn't putting any money down, and Cara was out to prove that she was nobody's fool.

MISTY MORNINGS, MAGIC NIGHTS
Ada Steward #319—July 1986
The last thing Carole Stockton wanted was to fall in love with another politician, especially Donnelly Wakefield. But under a blanket of secrecy, far from the campaign spotlights, their love became a powerful force.

AM-TRIB-1R

AMERICAN TRIBUTE

American Tribute titles now available:

RIGHT BEHIND THE RAIN
Elaine Camp #301—April 1986
The difficulty of coping with her brother's
death brought reporter Raleigh Torrence
to the office of Evan Younger, a police
psychologist. He helped her to deal with
her feelings and emotions, including love.

THIS LONG WINTER PAST
Jeanne Stephens #295—March 1986
Detective Cody Wakefield checked out
Assistant District Attorney Liann McDowell,
but only in his leisure time. For it was the
danger of Cody's job that caused Liann to
shy away.

LOVE'S HAUNTING REFRAIN
Ada Steward #289—February 1986
For thirty years a deep dark secret kept them
apart—King Stockton made his millions while
his wife, Amelia, held everything together.
Now could they tell their secret, could they
admit their love?

 **Silhouette Desire**

COMING NEXT MONTH

GREEN FIRE—Stephanie James
Was Rani's life endangered by inheriting an antique emerald ring? It was a fake—but the man who appeared on her doorstep was undeniably real. He claimed he was there to protect her....

DESIGNING HEART—Laurel Evans
Lighting director Stella Ridgeway was perfectly content with her career; playwright Sam Forster was quite happy being alone. But there was an undeniable magnetism between them that neither could resist!

BEFORE THE WIND—Leslie Davis Guccione
Disheartened after a bad marriage, Whitney was determined to avoid the pain of involvement again—until she met Paul. Paul helped her regain her self-esteem, but could she learn to love once more?

WILLING SPIRIT—Erin Ross
Athena MacKay went to Scotland to reclaim Kildrurry, "haunted" castle of her ancestors that had been stolen by the Burke clan. Christopher Burke was no ghost—but could she give her heart to the enemy?

THE BLOND CHAMELEON—Barbara Turner
Delancey was good at impersonating movie stars—and good at hiding her real self from the man she loved. But Stuart was intrigued, and insisted on finding the woman within.

CAJUN SUMMER—Maura Seger
Eight years ago, Arlette left the Louisiana bayou to pursue her own career. That had meant leaving Julian behind. Now she was back, and this time he wasn't going to let her go!

AVAILABLE THIS MONTH: